Adventure Turned to Despair

BEU ORIELS

Ordering Information:

Prime Seven Media
518 Landmann St.
Tomah City, WI 54660

Printed in the United States of America

TABLE OF CONTENTS

ADVENTURE TURNED TO DESPAIR 1

THE ENCOUNTER 6

DECEMBER- 15TH- 2004 8

IN SEARCH OF A TICKET 9

THE DEPARTURE 12

THE GOOD OMEN! 13

ON BOARD THE AIRCRAFT 14

DUBAI AIRPORT 18

TWO HOURS LATER - SHAJAH 21

THE NEXT DAY- DECEMBER 16TH 23

VITORIA 26

THE ATTRACTION 30

THURSDAY MORNING- 17TH DECEMBER 31

DUBAI – THE UNIQUE 35

CONTRARY PHASE TO GLAMOUR 36

IMPACT - THE GUEST 38

ARABIAN NIGHT LIFE 39

THEIR SURPRISE 41

AZIZ - THE NEIGHBOUR 42

A COUPLE OF HOURS LATER 43

THE JUMERIAH BEACH – DECEMBER 18TH, 2004 45

HAILEY LEAVES HER FRIENDS 47

DARING BUT IMPULSIVE...50

THE INVITATION..51

ON THE BOAT 53

ALL EYES SWEEP THE OCEAN 54

DISTRAUGHT WITH WORRY 56

FRIDAY – DECEMBER 18TH.2004 57

DECEMBER 19TH. 2004...60

IN THE YACHT 62

DECEMBER 20TH,2004..65

THE NIGHT...69

DECEMBER 21ST. 2004..77

REGRETS..80

THE NEW BEGINNING 81

HAILEY REALIZES HER SITUATION..............................85

OPPORTUNITY KNOCKS AT HER DOOR 88

THE REVELATION...89

THE SHOPPING SPREE...94

THE CONTACT 95

PREMEDITATED SHOPPING SPREE.............................98

RANI'S PRIORITY 101

THE PLOT 102

CHANGE OF PLANS 109

A BRAIN WAVE..111

FORGOTTEN PACKET 113

THE MESSAGE 115

CHANGE OF PLANS 116

THE PLAN 119

INSIDE THE AIRPORT 122

INTUITIVE ACTION 124

AFTER THE BELLY DANCE............................128

MISTAKE UNCOVERED 130

THE SUFI ZIKA 131

HAILEY IS MISSING 132

A CHANGE OF PLANS 135

THE ACCIDENT...136

THE CHAOS 137

AT THE HOSPITAL 140

REACTION OF EMBASSY.............................. 141

AZIZ – THE REACTION 142

AZIZ AT THE HOSPITAL 143

NEW ENCOUNTER..145

THE TURN OF EVENTS 146

ALICE AT THE EMBASSY 148

THE NEW CONNECTION 149

THE SUSPICION..150

THE REVELATION...153

STRANGE EPISODE 156

Adventure turned to Despair

*H*ailey Arlington wakes up in good spirits. She jumps out of bed on that cold winter morning filled with renewed energy. She was determined to shake off that dismal period of nearly a week wasted during her Christmas holidays. She lay curled up in bed running a temperature and facing the effects of a bad attack of flu.

I must pull myself together and try to make the most of the few golden days left before going back to work. Her thoughts took her back home when Christmas time was very special. Friends and families usually got together and held numerous parties.

She came from a family of five. Her father followed the regimental rules. Law and order was the norm- so study time was considered sacred besides all the other duties everyone had to follow. But this did not mean there was no play. In the evenings after duties, dinner and prayer, singing, music and dancing formed part of the routine. So they all turned out to be great dancers.

She brushes off her nostalgia. She decides to make that day an enjoyable day. No sooner than she draws the blinds the sun filters through the flimsy pink curtains, filling the room with streams of glowing sunlight, filling her with great excitement.

Being adventurous, a new experience is what she kept thinking would invigorate her! Just then the phone rings. She dashes down the stairs for it. She picks it up, only to see the smiling face of her dear friend Alice who lives in Dubai.

Hailey: A bit hoarse, she croaks, "Don't you look amazing! It is great to hear you, after such a long time. Your cheerful voice fills me with happiness. It seems as if your bright blast of sunshine has broken through the clouds, making my day."

Alice, "You sound like shit, babe what's wrong? I think it's time you took a break.

Hailey, "I was down with a bout of flu."

Alice: "Well now is the time for you to come to Dubai for a holiday. The Cultural festival is on so I thought this would be an irresistible opportunity for you. You are so involved in the World of Art. Artists from all over the world would be attending. The whole city is getting dressed up for the occasion.

Well here's the great offer sitting under your nose… the Cultural Festival is being held during this time from the twenty-sixth of December, to the eighth of January.

Bursting with excitement, Alice could see and hear Hailey dancing and jumping around.

Hailey: "Yes! Yes! That would mean realizing one of my greatest dreams!"

"You not only sound awful but look crappy! You surely need a reality check and wake up to the great things awaiting you. How much longer are you going to let your energy sleep? We haven't heard from you for over a fortnight. Don't you think it's time you took a break, my dear workaholic."

Hailey is a dedicated teacher. She works six hours a day in a High School in quite the toughest surroundings. She enjoys working with these teenagers although there are times when she finds them challenging.

Most of them came from broken homes or messy environments. But she loved them and went out of her way to make them feel very special by trying to bring out the very best in them. Often they work as a team. Now and again she had to put her foot down when they got out of hand and lay down the rules before she got trodden on.

Now this was an enormous gate, opening to an unexpected opportunity that she would never have thought about. Her eyes glazed for a moment as if looking clearly back on the curve of her life. She realises that there was no more time to waste and would no longer sacrifice her great desires. It was time to live a little! Dubai, a city of adventure and contrast, she was told. A new experience would help brighten her otherwise drab life.

She was rather impulsive and naïve sometimes. But she was alive and spread cheer wherever she went.

"No more time to waste!" She shouted excitedly. "Now is the time to be adventurous. A new experience is what would invigorate me! Risk is better than boredom so here I go, a new me, beginning today!"

Alice interrupts her thoughts. "We will make sure you have a wonderful time. You should get out…. rather escape from that drudgery, empty life you lead. Now don't come out with that usual excuse –Pierre's afraid of flying, after his trip from Seattle to Pasco and all that turbulence….poor baby!"

Hailey, "It all sounds very exciting.

Alice, "Leave your husband alone in peace. That's what he needs but for you it's high time you broke free and put some colour into your life."

Hailey: "I guess there is a deadline to register?"

Alice, "That's exactly why I called, to give you some vital information. I just thought that this is something extraordinary. I didn't want you to waste any time, so I actually went one step ahead and got the registration forms for you. I shall e-mail them to you, right away."

Hailey, "Did you? That is really amazing, rather quite a call for action then. No two ways about it. I have been dormant for a long time."

Alice: "So what you have to do now is to fill in these forms with your details and send it back to me A.S.A.P."

Hailey: "Well I can hardly wait to receive them!"

Alice: "Let's do it right away. A couple of minutes right now, and you are done. I repeat, right now. As Nike says, "Just do it!" This way, there is no room for doubts, neither for procrastination."

Hailey: "Oooo…la….la. I am getting really excited.

Alice: "Besides, being the early bird, gets you the privilege of choosing an outstanding space at the exhibition. Of course there is a success tax involved. If you wish everyone to see your work this is going to be your best option."

The moment she hangs up she listens to her heart and let it sing. And she actually began singing as she waltzes down to her little office in the house and opens her computer. She sees the forms, scans through it and then fills in the required forms. Without wasting any time she e-mails it right way to Alice.

Alice: "Wow! Congratulations! You are surely fired up! And that is the way to go. So I am doing the same. Your forms will reach them any moment as I am sending it right away to them."

ᏖHE ᏋNᏟOᏌNᏖᏋR

*H*ailey meets Alice and Tony at Pacos Tapas Restaurant, in the Rioja. It is considered the wine country of Spain - The Rioja. Their wines are considered, one of the best in the world. It forms part of the Basque Country as they call it, although it is very much part of Spain.

This is where they used to go often in their earlier days, when they had come on a holiday to Spain a couple of years ago. It happened to be Pierre's 42nd birthday. Hailey couldn't resist interrupting them when she overhears them speak in English. They were sitting at a table right next to them.

Hailey: "I may sound rude butting in like this, but I could not help eavesdropping, listening to you speaking in English raised my curiosity. It is pretty unusual here. It would be a great pleasure to invite you to join us, at our table, if you'd like to." Later she invited them over to her place. They agreed and since have become very good friends.

They had dinner together and since it was a Friday evening, she remembered the days gone by when they were very sociable and went out a lot. She coaxed Pierre to take them out.

Most of the people go bar- hopping after dinner till literally dawn. Hailey and Pierre, had lost practise, in doing something like this, in a long, long, time.

Hailey: "Let us show our new-found, friends the night life in Vitoria. This was a great excuse for Hailey to convince her husband who normally went to bed by 10:00p.m.

Since then Alice and Hailey maintained their friendship.

December 15th 2004

*N*ow that she had made up her mind, Hailey did not waste any time. She was off to the travel agents hoping to pick up a ticket to suit her pocket.

They had just invested quite a great deal on the renovation, of the house. She knew that Pierre was going to make a noise about it, but she just didn't care.

She realised that this was an unexpected expense they hadn't counted on. But the great excitement that kept mounting and creeping through her body made her tremble. She visualizes herself doing exactly what she really wanted and what she needed at that moment.

IN SEARCH OF A TICKET

*E*verywhere she went she was told, "It is high season. Besides a last minute ticket is much more expensive so you either pay an exorbitant price or forget your trip!"

Money! Money! Often kept her from reaching out to what the Universe was offering her and made her doubt before taking action. But now she was determined to follow her heart. Neither did she have a choice, really.

She realised that she had just chosen the most exclusive area and size of the space for her exhibition, for which she had already paid for. There was no turning back now, on her commitment to exhibit her works of Art in Dubai. Just the thought filled her with exhilaration.

Shopping around for a last minute ticket could be harassing as they are usually exorbitant. She decided to sleep over it after visiting a couple of travel agents. She didn't have a choice but she had to go ahead one way or another. This was fulfilling one of her greatest dreams.

On waking up early, the next day a little worm kept nibbling into her brain …The little voice kept saying -Go to the agent who was quite some distance away. Well it's now or never she thought and rightly enough fortune smiles on her!

A reasonably priced ticket that suited her pocket is what she found. Without giving it another thought she purchased it.

She was now filled with a power that seemed like jolts of electricity. She just had a couple of days to send her works after having her paintings accepted by the committee.

Now this was a very special moment. She had to make the right choice, when it came to exhibiting her work. She went through her numerous paintings. Finally she decided on three of them which felt would capture the interest of a wide audience.

One of them was mostly blue with a touch of beige and gold. It was one of her extraordinary achievements. It was quite an interesting mixture of water with oil paints, pretty unusual combination and a difficult one, too.

At first it looks as if someone had splashed the canvas with a can of paint with the added water that drips and spreads in all directions, without any taste or design.

Hailey: "By the way, I usually dance, to Rock n' roll or allow classical music to enter the Magic Nation where my imagination carries me into unknown world. For that matter, any music that drives my senses to the point when it brings out the best, the happiest moments of my life. The kind of music depends largely on the moment.

Going back to this specific painting she continues.

Hailey "I work on it, enjoying the feel of the paint on the tips of her fingers as it spreads in different directions taking form very slowly as different figures jump out here and there, coming to life.

I don't often use traditional brushes. Sticks, caps, and any object that could help take different forms at that specific moment. I work with a broad range of mediums and material, enjoying the play with paints and inks on canvas or photographic paper.

Hailey: "It's exciting to allow the ink to flow and fall, mix and dance its own way."

GHE DEPARGURE

Hailey: "Today is my grand day!"

She was up at dawn. She watches the sun as it slowly begins to peek over the horizon. She stays there, by the window as always looking forward to grab the light and the warmth of the morning sun. She did a moment later. She feels its caress as the first rays of golden light filters through the trees and hits the windows of her terrace filling it with a great resplendent light.

Hailey always gets carried away by nature's bounty. She is thrilled to watch the moon in all its phases and enjoys Star-gazing. Three years ago she went up to the mountains in Tenerife at 3715mts to watch the amazing night sky. Recently she grabs the opportunity of joining a couple of Astro-physicists and goes up to the mountains in Asturias, the North of Spain 1600mts.to enjoy the summer night sky from midnight to around 4a.m.

тне good omen!

ooking at the mirror, she turns around, now left, then right, to make sure she looked her very best. Shaking her golden tresses that were ablaze with the morning sun, she grabs her bag. She checks to make sure she has her ticket and passport.

Just then she hears, Pierre's impatient shout, "Are you coming down or not?"

She decides to keep her cool although she was terribly nervous. Without much ado, she says a wee prayer and dashes down to the car. Before entering the car, she checked to see that all her bags were inside.

He is normally very punctual and rather impatient but organized. He made sure that her bags were on the ground floor, the night before.

The moment he sets his eyes on her, he gets a bit ticked off. He didn't quite, like the idea, of being left alone in the house.

Hailey was a bit nervous, too. It showed! A tear or two rolls down her face. She quickly brushes it off, not wanting him to see it. For a moment she was filled with remorse having to leave him behind.

She couldn't restrain the tears before she kissed him goodbye. She felt like a child leaving home for the first time.

ON BOARD THE AIRCRAFT

Half an hour later she was on board. Her eyes sparkle with emotion. She feels an explosion burst within her, she couldn't control.

She looks out of the window. She muses on the events of the last years of her life. She had endured years of a passionless marriage, craving for a man's loving touch which was lost.

All the tender loving care of the staff made her feel very special. This was her day. There was something about her that either attracted people to her or caused great envy. Here fortune smiled on her. She was not only up graded to first class but …..

A few moments later a fine looking gentleman was shown to his seat, right beside her. The deference showed to him, proved he must have been someone of distinction.

Later she was told that he was a renowned heart surgeon from India and well known in Dubai. He turned out to be a very pleasant companion to travel with.

Hailey, "This was quite an amazing experience, for me- indelible to say, the least. He spoke about one of his experiences that made a great impression on me. It took place in his private clinic.

Dr, Ajit: "On one occasion, one of my patients had a cardiac arrest. His heart stopped beating for about 35minutes- in medical history, he is supposed to be, clinically dead. His heart collapses, after his heart operation. We then use the defibrillator to sends electric shocks to restore a normal heart beat ad gave him CPR but we could not bring him back. All our efforts seemed to be in vain.

But I kept at it. One of the surgeons: "He is dead. There's nothing we can do for him, Dr. Ajit, please, please- leave him alone. You have done all that's within your reach. I know he is your best friend- face the reality of the situation."

But I was far gone in the sense I wasn't listening to him nor to the surroundings, but to my heart.

Dr. Aji, his eyes closed, re-living those moments he continues, "but I didn't, I couldn't give up, I knew I could still do something to revive him and decided to do one last CPR and held on to his hand real tight. You see, this patient was one of my best friends. I just could not give up on him. I kept breathing in and out, very slowly and praying with my heart and soul, for his revival. Suddenly I felt a pull from the patient."

Hailey interrupts, taking a deep breath she says, "Incredible!"

Overcome with emotion, she holds out her hand to him and gives it a reassuring squeeze, as if it was happening at that precise moment and she was sitting beside him, there. Tears steam down his cheeks, as he seems to re-live those moments.

Dr. Ajit, "Surprisingly enough he recovers with no signs of injury physically nor mentally which is incomprehensible, in medical history. The brain is the most powerful where miracles and strange healing activities occur.

Hailey's eyes fill with tears, too- she could not control.

Dr. Ajit: "One of the mysteries of life, which at times has no explanation! So, you must have faith. It's like a flash-light – no matter how things seem to get, it will find a way. It's tough, practical and realistic! It sees the invisible, it doesn't see the non-existent." He re-instated.

Hailey: "It was a great learning experience for me…to have faith even in the impossible!"

Dr. Ajit: "The patient who was a sixty year old, with other medical issues suddenly jerks my hand." He squeaks in a low voice, "You are hurting my hand! Why are you holding on to it so tight?"

Dr. Ajit, "My body trembles with excitement."

Relaxed, he smiles and says: "All we did at that moment was to break out into hearty laughter. Not before I once again whispered a wee prayer of thanksgiving."

Dr. Ajit : "Oh! I am so sorry if I hurt you. I did not mean to do so," he laughingly said to his patient.

Hailey: "It was a privilege to be in his company. There was something very special about him. He was a great conversationalist, deep sometimes but also had time for jokes. So time just flew. Besides the differential treatment he received, he made sure that I was part of it."

So I got to savour all the delicacies he had been served.

DUBAI AIRPORT

Hailey is taken aback on her arrival at the airport. She feels lost for a moment, wondering whether she would find her way around. It is easy for that to happen in such an enormous airport.

Global Village, Dubai International Airport is the primary international airport serving Dubai, United Arab Emirates. It is one of the world's busiest airports by international passenger traffic. It is so enormous that it has more than 50 gates, providing very well-equipped facilities. The airport is amazing and impeccable.

It has received international acclaim for its outstanding health and safety standards. The recognition comes from the Royal Society for the Prevention of Accidents (RoSPA) and marks the second year that Global Village has earned this prestigious Gold RoSPA Leisure Safety Award- an acknowledgement of excellence especially for businesses that serve visitors. This ensures the safety and well-being of visitors and partners.

Her worries were soon brushed aside. A great surprise awaits her. The Welcome Committee, in charge of the Cultural Art Festival had a placard with her name on it. Anita Suresh approached her with a bouquet of flowers.

Anita: "Come this way. It is a great pleasure to meet you. Your luggage will be taken care of."

Taken aback, she discovers that they wave all airport bureaucracy. They surely knew how to make one feel very special and that's what I felt as most of the officers at the Customs wore a welcome smile-incredible isn't it?

Once outside, they hand over her bags to her friends who approached her, hugging and kissing her.

Anita turns to Hailey's friends a-waiting to pick her up. "You will have to spare her for an hour or so. We will drop her back at your place. We have your address."

She's whisked away as another member, with hands outstretched, "So you are the Artist from Spain. We have been looking forward, to meeting you. We are here to give you a short but sweet introduction to our city."

"It is our great pleasure, to have you amongst us. Your paintings are extraordinary. We placed them in an enviable position. We are sure that everyone entering the Festival will be attracted to it. You did well, to send in your work as fast as you did. So you are one of our first exhibitors." Added Anjou

The Secretary joins in, "We have prepared a cocktail. You will be meeting all the Artists from all corners of the world. So enjoy."

Once everyone was seated, the president came on to the podium and gave a short, simple speech. He explained all the procedures to be followed by the Artists. He gave them a whole-hearted welcome that made everyone there feel very special.

After all the introductions to the members who were responsible for the success of the Cultural Festival, he invited everyone to the adjoining room. Here there was a toast and cold fruit juices were served with delectable snacks.

There was a great deal of excitement as all the Artists began introducing themselves to each other. Hailey was pleased to meet other artists. Many of them made a point of wearing their traditional costumes of their country which to her was an added novelty.

She got talking two of the artists who were sitting next to her. One of them was from Israel….(Name her) and another from Los Angeles. He was actually a renowned scientist. ….name him. But he explained how much Art helped him relax and think with clarity after a heavy day's work.

Ellie Griva: "Hello, I live in Greece but I came in a couple of days ago and got to visit the preparation going on at the EXPO. I was very keen on meeting you as your work impressed me greatly.

two hours later
~ shajah

Great expectations fill her as she realises that this was going to be a new and exciting experience! And what an indelible experience!

That evening they spoke until rather late, trying to catch up with all that had happened in each of their lives. To their surprise, she showed no signs of a jetlag. The excitement of being with her friend was so great they couldn't stop jabbering.

Hailey: "Although I am tired it is better to fall in with your timings right from the beginning. I guess I will also sleep better."

Alice: "Then let's take you out for just an hour or two."

That evening they stroll along the paths and gardens that lined a circular body of water. There were numerous benches for people to sit and relax or enjoy the neon lights of the city that kept shimmering on the water

A 100 metre water-fall shoots up, now and again in the nearby creek, to a play of coloured lights. This usually took place every half an hour or so when all the surrounding lights slowly flicked into life.

Alice: "This usually comes on after dusk, around seven in the evening."

Hailey and Alice had been friends for a couple of years. They were both of the same height 5ft-4"tall. They could pass off as sisters. Both had sparkling blue eyes and blonde hair but Hailey had dimples on her cheeks. She was slim, supple with a lithe body unlike while Alice was on the heavy side.

Both were lively. They shared the same tastes and above all enjoyed dancing very much. Alice and her friends were all party goers. But Hailey did not have that opportunity, very much. Pierre was not one for parties so she hadn't been to one for a long, long time.

THE NEXT DAY-
DECEMBER 16TH

She was up when the sun slowly peeked over the horizon. She watched it as it began to come up. An instant later she felt the caress of its golden light as she opened the door to the balcony. The day dawned bright and beautiful.

Hailey was born in a seaside town in the south of Spain called Benidorm. Her parents moved here from London after they had retired.

It is a resort on the eastern coast of Spain, part of the Valencia region's famed Costa Blanca. It used to be a tiny fishing village till 1960s. It is now a popular Mediterranean holiday destination for its nightlife. Many people from Britain retire here. They come in search of a warm climate and the colourful ambience that goes with it. Most retirees enjoy this weather away from the wet and humidity that could be quite long-drawn and dreary in winter.

Its two wide sandy beaches, Levante Beach and Poniente Beach are backed by palm-lined promenades, bars and rows of skyscrapers.

Hailey met Pierre at one of the discos in Benidorm where he had been spending his holidays with some of his friends. His light eyes and debonair looks drew her attention. His exclusive taste of clothes that fell beautifully on him added to his attraction- Women were drawn to him like bees to honey.

She recalls the day when he, with a mischievous look on his face, approaches her, boldly asking for her telephone number with a girl hanging on to his arm.

This brought laughter to her heart, which she couldn't show, so she kept it under control. Hailey had a great sense of humour. She considered it a hell of a joke and was tickled pink by the situation. She readily agreed to his request much to the rebuff of her friends who protested profusely as they could not contain their fury at his audacity.

"Who the hell does he think he is, to approach you like that?" Mierda! Vaya cara dura! She swore in Spanish. If I were you I wouldn't have given him my number!" Another interrupts, "how dare he come to you like that?"

The moment they see her give her number to him, a couple of them nudge each other, showing their clear disapproval....Tonta! Vaya Tonta! Completely stupid behaviour!

Maria, "You are crazy, can't you see the type of guy he is, shameless to the core! He is known to be notorious amongst women and easily captures many who are stupid enough to fall for his charms. How can you do something like this?"

What her friends did not realise was that Hailey sort of found the situation pretty hilarious and decided to play his game with a laugh in her heart. She wasn't one bit keen on him at that time. Unaware, of her attraction, she drew numerous admirers. So really this wasn't any different! She thought little of it!

She was equally daring and this could have been the deciding point of bringing them together, much unknown to either of them, at that moment. They were attracted to each other and before long he invited her over to the town where he was living, Vitoria.

VITORIA

Vitoria in the Basque country, was founded in 1181. Vitoria-Gasteiz is the capital of the Basque Autonomous community in northern Spain. About 240,000 people currently live here. In the medieval quarter, the Gothic-style Santa Maria Cathedral features a sculpted façade and towering columns. The 17TH Century Plaza de la Virgin Blanca has a monument to the 1813 Battle of Vitoria.

The Peninsular War, 1808-1813 Frustrated by Portugal's defiance of his Continental Blocade against trade with Great Britain, Napoleon ordered General Jerot to march French troops over the Pyrenees. He was determined to bend the Spanish people, he had decided to make Spain part of his Empire.

Napoleon could never imagine that some people loved their countries as much as he loved his own. It was a failing, compounded by arrogance and pride that brought his downfall. At the Battle of Vitoria (21June 1813) a British, Portuguese and Spanish army under the Marquis of Wellington broke the French army under King Joseph Bonaparte and Marshal Jean- Baptiste Jourdan near Vitoria, eventually leading to victory in the Peninsular War. It was the last major battle against Napoleon's forces in Spain and opened the way for the British forces under Lord Wellington to invade France.

They began dating and often enough he would be quite the stalker, following her everywhere, unknown to her. It looked as if it was love at first sight and they couldn't be separated.

A couple of months later they decided to get married.

He realised it was time to introduce her to his mother who was living in another province.

His mother had other plans for her son and didn't quite take too kindly to welcoming a foreigner into the home.

The moment he walked into the house and introduced Hailey to his mother, she decided to fake a dizzy spell and fell on to the floor, hoping her son would see her displeasure and fall in with her desire.

But to her great despair and surprise, he turned as if to walk away.

Turning to Hailey, he held out his hand saying, "Come on, let's go. We are not welcome here!"

Within the second she resurrected.

His mother: "Please don't leave!" She kept pleading. From then she was pretty sweet and made sure Hailey felt welcome. But in the meantime Hailey decided to give the mother and son some time together.

She quietly slipped out through the door. But to her surprise she was not alone. The curious neighbours awaited her, outside. They were quite friendly and tried their best to converse with her.

Hailey, "Although my command of Spanish wasn't very good I had an added problem. In his home town, the North-west of Spain called Galicia they spoke a dialect that's between Portuguese and Spanish, called Gallego. It was rather difficult to understand especially with the strong accent of the people in the village.

She felt fortunate that they seemed to have taken to her instantly.

Hailey: "We actually had quite a long conversation. Most often I couldn't follow what they were saying, but made as if I understood everything by observing their facial expressions very carefully and joining in their laughter. They really kept me entertained until such time they led me back to the house. They gave us the best. And I felt pretty comfortable.

She wasn't sure whether she made a fool of herself as often enough her command of the language was not as strong as they supposed it was, and she had to pretend to understand all that they were saying. Her dictionary was her great support so it didn't take long before she slowly became fluent in the language.

Now in the villages they wake up very early to attend to their animals and due to the cold they usually had this alcoholic drink which for them was a wake-up drink and warm –up drink. It is a special home-made liqueur. It had a fruity taste, but it was a pretty strong drink - for the first thing to down on waking up.

Hailey: "This was way too strong for me, especially early in the morning when I would have welcomed my tea and longed for one, which wasn't coming!" She learned to accept alcohol very politely and made sure there was a plant beside her so could help it get drunk. She would toss it out rather than hurt someone's feelings. Alcohol was pretty much the norm among most of her companions. It was all the more difficult for her to have something like that on an empty stomach.

the attraction

*T*heir attraction was mutual. They settled down to a happy married life, there. They had two children Elena and Enrique. Before long they left their nest and Hailey discovers that her life was a mere monotony.

It reached a point it was just cooking and cleaning. One day she woke up to the reality that she had reached the limits where she would go over and over the flooring making sure it shone like a mirror. Often worried about staining the floor, she actually wore a special type of slippers – towel-like, for her feet so she would be constantly shining the floor each time she walked over it.

Pierre was a kind of a hermit, hardy, five ft. 9 inches tall short blonde hair. It didn't take long before his hair receded forming a crown around his balding head that shone like the crescent of the first quarter, moon.

He was happy tinkering around his workshop, doing some gardening or watching football. So every Friday evening they were off to their little cottage in the Rioja - the wine country in the North of Spain.

THURSDAY MORNING- 17TH DECEMBER

Around eleven on Thursday morning, Malcolm and Alice decided to show her around the city. Hailey was dazzled as they drove around the Central Business District of Dubai stopping to visit the busy souks and admiring the intricate work of the immaculate white Mosque. Her eyes sparkled as it switched from one direction to the other. This was an ultra-modern city with skyscrapers which seemed to be competing with each other. They were taller than any seen in New York.

The Grand Mosque, originally built in 1900 was re- built in 1960 and once again in 1998. It is located between the textile souk and the Dubai Museum close to a small stream in the BUR Dubai area. It now holds up to 1200 worshippers.

Non-Muslims are permitted to enter the Mosque daily from Sunday to Thursday. The mosque is the hub of Dubai's religious and cultural life. The height of the Minaret rises to 70meters. It is called The Iranian (Garashi)Hosainia Mosque.

The waterfront was dominated by impressive, glass- clad buildings around the marina.

The creek was lined by distinct form of boats called Abras – the traditional Dhows – their national pride and Emblem. Not surprising! The Old with the New! The People of Dubai went directly, from the camel, to the Cadilac ! As the saying, goes. This is one of the outstanding differences between other cities in the world.

The history of the UAE is diverse and immersive. Tales of Nomadic Arabs, or Bedouins, who once inhabited the region was very popular. They are known for their lifestyle and hardy resourcefulness, they are an intrinsic part of the region and its heritage.

Bedouins were known for their nomadic lifestyles in the desert. Bedouin herders used to dwell in the area of a mangrove swamp in Dubai between 2500 BCE and 3000BCE and engaged in date palm cultivation. Even today live in tents across the desert terrain. These tents could have two to five sections- known as Bawahir, with a different number of poles supporting them. The higher the number of divisions and poles in the tent, the richer the owner was considered.

Their tents were of average height and made of goat hair. In some cases long strips sheqaq were used to form the roof of the tent. While crafting tents, they ensured to choose a type of cloth that withstands the seasonal and extreme weather conditions.

During summers, these tents could draw the air out from the inside and create a cooling effect, and become water-resilient and tighter when it rained or snowed during winters.

They make shoes from animal skins, primarily of goat and camel. While the shoes protected them from the hot desert, sand bags helped them store milk, water and many dairy products. Additionally, they used animal hair to make rugs, blankets, camel, horse trappings and carpets with intricate designs and beautiful colour patterns. Their carpet weaving is very much alive today.

Moreover, the traditional embroidery form of AL- Sadu or Sadu is hand-woven by them.

They primarily consume rice and food items made of flour, while also relishing tea, nuts, dried fruits and goat meat. They cook food on campfires.

Goat milk is a popular beverage consumed after boiling it with thyme and salt for seasoning. They make butter and buttermilk by churning milk in a bag made of animal skin. They also use the buttermilk- laban to make thick cheese and clarified butter-samn

They make their clothes from the wool of animals. Their clothes are both practical and fashionable, designed to keep them comfortable in the extreme hot summers and cold desert winters. While men wear loose-fitting white tunics with a head-cloth and cloak, women preferred loose, flowy garments decorated with different patterns and protected by a special cover.

They have a wide range of interests and skills. Falconry is a popular sport in the UAE. During hunting, they capitalised on the natural abilities of falcons. The birds are strong, speedy and dexterous- so a hunting tool. They train and tame the falcons to hunt hare, birds and other preys. Camel Racing is used in show contests. Often camel racing and beauty contests take place together.

Star-gazing is another very important activity.

Nabati Poetry has a long-standing tradition among them which is considered an integral part of their culture.

Bedouins are known for their values of loyalty and honour. They are faithful to their families, clans and tribes. While the men hunt, trade and protect the family, women took care of the household.

Their key trait of the host is hospitality. They treat guests with utmost respect making sure that every need of theirs is fulfilled and share food, coffee, dates and dry fruits with them.

Al Marmoon is a popular example of the Bedouin experience amidst the golden sand dunes.

DUBAI - THE UNIQUE

ubai is a kind of unimaginable, wonder-land, always making sure their imagination takes wings to create the nearly impossible. It has the world's largest natural, incredible, amazing, flower garden.

It is about 72,000sq.miles. It measures about ten football fields. It is referred to as Dubai's Miracle Garden, which is a Florist's dream. The floral display with about 50 million natural flowers, are in all forms and shapes ranging from life-like animals, birds to houses, castles, Disney characters, an aeroplane and hanging gardens and anything unimaginable.

An ultra-Modern city, the culture intricately tied validating their financial superiority and humility, in their approach to make tourists from all over the world feel very much at home with their hospitality.

CONTRARY PHASE TO GLAMOUR

On the contrary to the glamour of the city, there are stories of migrant workers being ill-treated. Now this could depend on who employs them. Many cut-throat companies, who are out and out, just for the money, do not respect their workers.

These workers are mostly Asians who are terrorised and dare not complain. They fear of being been thrown into prison. Sometimes this happens for no rhyme, or reason and completely forgotten. The legal system is young and is far from competent. They sometimes live in pathetic conditions. At times twelve people sleep and share the same room. The toilets are far cry from cleanliness and health-related issues. Their passports are withheld so this lack of freedom keeps them tied to their despicable bosses with no opportunity to move from one company to another.

Most of these workers belong to Asian and South Eastern Asian community blue-collar workers are in this situation. The Europeans and The North Americans are highly respected and receive high salaries. All this boiled down to whom you worked for. Numerous companies came from all over the world. Most often workers were treated well but in such situations you also find cut-throats who exploited their workers. This happens in many parts of the world.

ímpact - the guest

*U*nknown to Hailey most of the friendly neighbours in their block observe her. Some of them, mostly women, do not work. They were pretty bored so their time was spent in their terraces. They were very friendly too. Her arrival aroused their curiosity and a couple of them were very keen on meeting her.

Above all, she created a great impact on Akbar Aziz. He was tall, of swarthy complexion, with an air of aristocratic elegance.

Hailey captured his attention. She was very different in many ways from her friends. Her cheerful character mixed with the Spanish influence made her outstanding. Her sun-kissed, British skin added to her beauty. Hailey was bright-spirited, bouncy and charming. Her fatal flaw - she was, naïve and unsuspecting. She was unaware of her enticing beauty. Filled with euphoria of the moment she ventures into an alien world, way beyond her control.

Aziz was filled with a smouldering passion the moment he set his dark-eyed, gaze on her. All the more observing her child-like exhuberance pulled at his heartstrings. He was determined to find a way of getting to meet her.

ARABIAN NIGHT LIFE

That night Alice decides to give Hailey a taste of the Arabian Night. They first took her to the Exclusive, restaurant in town- Gordon Ramsay Hell's Kitchen – Dubai -the second in the world, after Las Vegas. A multi- Michelin- starred chef.

They explained that the food served here included a speciality Beef wellington, Eggs in Purgatory and the Sweet Heavenly Sticky Toffee pudding.

Hailey: "It sounds like a very exclusive place and very American. If you don't mind I would rather go to an exotic, very typical Arab Restaurant.

The exclusive restaurant they had originally planned to take her was in the Caesar's Palace Dubai. It looked too very exclusive and expensive and for her taste. She realized it would cost them a fortune. And this was not that she really cared for.

Hailey: "Frankly speaking I would like to experience the real life here and to have food where normal people go a dinner and have a typical meal.

Alice: "We know of a place you are surely going to like."

It was one of those, perfect, deliciously warm Thursday evenings. The air on your cheeks felt like silk. The temperature was just a refreshing 18° - a welcome break after the -10° at home, thought Hailey. The deep blue skies studded with stars added to it's unique character.

They sat under this canopy – the deep-blue starry sky enjoying the diversity of the Arab Cuisine until the early hours of the morning.

They had pilaf rice which had many aromatic spices, onion, tomatoes, dried lemon, lamb, pistachio and raisins. A variety of dips and a cold salad came with it.

She discovered that most of the people used the hookah – a smoking pipe with a long flexible tube, then, the smoke is drawn through water in vase to which tube and bowl are attached. She decided she wanted a taste of it but ended up coughing.

They were about to order their dessert when one of the waiters approached their table.

THEIR SURPRISE

"Compliments, from Mr.Aziz !"He pointed to the next table. Aziz nodded with a low bow, holding his palms together. They acknowledged him.

Aziz was slim and tall. His clothes fell well on his athletic body. Always elegant and impeccable but he was also very kind in his approach to everyone around him. He was much appreciated in the block of flats where nearly everyone were under the mistaken impression that he was just the manager in charge of those blocks of flats.

He always had a kind work for everyone and helpful in solving any problem. His humble approach gave people the impression that he was only the manager and not the rich business man who was the owner of all the surrounding blocks of ten buildings in that area called – Shajah.

They were presented with with a tray of the Arabian delicacy - Al –halwa, a sweet made with sugar, eggs, starch, water, pistachio and coconut oil.

AZIZ - THE NEIGHBOUR

Aziz is very friendly. I have known him for about six months. But this! Wow! This is amazing! Haven't you made an impression on him - your first conquest!......Just one day here and....this surely takes the cake.

They were all taken by surprise, but very pleased at such great attention shown to them.

A COUPLE OF
HOURS LATER

"I think I've had too much to dine. I can smell the sea. How about going for a ride along the waterfront?" Hailey said dreamily.

"That's no problem!" said Malcolm.

They drove for about half a kilometre. Malcolm parks beside the palm trees that lined the marina. They were not the only people who did so. It was pretty crowded with people. Flocks of people kept walking along the marina enjoying the bracing air of the late evening as the breezes blew from the surrounding nearby sea.

Most people in Dubai go out after their prayers on Thursday evenings - a kind of prelude to Friday. It is a holiday and a holy day. So the streets and restaurants were full. It was six in the morning!

They walked along until Hailey 's attention was drawn to this billowing, sail- shaped structure. "Does that outstanding structure represent anything special? That is unusual and beautiful. I have never seen something like that before!"

"That is the Burj Al Arab, the seven –star hotel. It soars, 321mts. above the Arabian Gulf. It's a dramatic tribute to the Regions ' seafaring heritage combining the latest technology with long-standing reputation of the Arabian Hospitality. The Hold symbolises the very essence of Dubai. It embraces the best of the new alongside the tradition of the past." Dolton explained.

Hailey was captivated by its uniqueness. It's grandeur could be seen from all directions. For a moment she wondered what it would be like to be within!

Her wildest dreams would not have prepared her when her wish is fulfilled.

the Jumeriah beach
- December 18ᵗʰ, 2004

T he next day her friends decided to take a day off. So they planned a picnic on the Jumeriah Beach.

Most of the people not only enjoyed walking along the refreshing tree-lined marina but held picnics there under the palm trees. Here there were numerous benches and tables for families to spend an enjoyable day.

That day friends of Alice also joined them. They were seven Dolton, Esther, their daughter Deah, Tina, Malcolm and Tony.

Each of them brought a hamper. They had some Typical, Arab dishes - dishes of the Emirates. Giant pita bread with falafel – seasoned ground beans. Then it was Shawarama sliced meat layered with slabs of fat into a vertical rotisserie with some salad, followed by a great variety of dates and cardamom laced coffee. And of course they enjoyed carrying their music with them. That was a must for them.

After lunch they usually play cards. It was a routine, something they enjoyed very much.

But Hailey couldn't see herself sitting down to something mundane like this. That was too sedentary for an active and energetic person as Hailey. This was unheard of in her world. Her friends had no idea how much she hated it. So, she found a plausible excuse to escape that situation.

HAILEY LEAVES HER FRIENDS

*H*ailey: "I hope you don't mind but I'd rather walk along the waterfront while you enjoy your game. The sea is my passion. I have always loved the sea. Since leaving my hometown I rarely get the opportunity of walking along the waterfront. This deep blue sea looks so alluring."

They readily agreed realising the enthusiasm Hailey displayed as she excused herself.

Hailey was wearing a pair of blue shorts and a t-shirt. Swim-suits, was not the norm in this beach. Her soft blue sandals gave her all that she needed to be comfortable in the water.

The sea was irresistible. Waiflike she prances around and goes splashing about as the waves lashed against the shore. The temperature of the water was a soothing 19 degrees.

"This is just amazing weather in winter!" She says loudly.

This environment fills her with happiness. She loved the sea. This enviable temperature added to its attraction.

Unknown to her she was being observed, by this tall gentleman dressed in an impeccable white tunic.

He was accompanied by two very attractive women. They had dark, big almond shaped eyes and jet-black hair. Both of them looked very friendly as they approached. One was wearing a lime-green kurta- a two piece pant outfit and the other a raw-silk outfit.

They kept smiling as they came towards her.

Jumma: "Excuse me, I hope you don't mind us disturbing your peace and enjoyment. We could not help being attracted by your cute, rather child-like, antics in the water so we couldn't resist approaching you. I am not surprised that my husband has been attracted to you. So were we. It is very clear that you are not from here. Do you mind if I ask you where you are from?

They kept plying her with questions in a friendly, manner. They introduced themselves, Sarita, Jumma and Akbar Aziz. We are from Afghanistan. We have been living here for the past six months and we love it here.

Aziz kept in the background. She realised that he was the gentleman at the restaurant. He was the one who kindly got her to taste their delicious dessert, the night before. It was clear that neither of the ladies were aware of it. He was in the restaurant with a group of friends. So she evaded the subject.

Sarita: We saw you arrive the other day. We live in Shajah, too. Alice and Malcolm are just opposite our apartment and we are well acquainted with them. We recognised a couple of their friends. But we would not like to disturb their card game, at this moment. Maybe we could join them after our boat-ride.

DARING BUT IMPULSIVE

*I*t didn't take long before Hailey felt very much at home with them. She recognized the gentleman who had invited them to a tray of delicious Arab sweets.

Jumma casually mentioned she was an artist. Since Hailey was an artist, their mutual interest brought them closer. She felt very comfortable. They discussed some of their work.

Jumma: "Well we must find some time together. I would love to show you my work and get your opinion. I have never exhibited them before. And yes your ideas would be very welcome.

Jumma was excited to share those moments with someone she felt had the same taste as her.

Hailey: "That would be wonderful! I would like that, too. I could also learn something from you."

She readily agreed as this was an added opportunity to learn the influence of Art in different cultures.

All this while, Aziz kept in the background. He enjoyed observing her.

He could not wait any longer. This was his opportunity!

ᏦᎻᎬ ᎥᏁᏉᎥᏖᎪᏖᎥᎾᏁ

"Well girls since we were planning on going for a speedboat ride why don't we invite this young lady to join us, too. I am sure Malcolm and Alice won't mind as I know them very well. "He interrupted.

He made it a point to study each of the families who rented his condos.

"Everyone does it here especially on a gorgeous day like today!" The ladies added in unison!"

Taken aback by their kind invitation, at first she doubted but on second thoughts they seemed so very friendly. She also remembered the desert of the day before…extremely kind!

Hailey: "Why not?" She thought, "This sounds exciting!"

She had been observing the boats and noticed that they usually didn't go for more than a twenty, minute ride. She jumps at the idea but not before she decides to tell her friends. So she bellows out to them.

Hailey: "I am going for a speedboat ride with these wonderful friends of yours!"

She recalls the restaurant and took it for granted that Aziz was a well-known friend of Alice and Malcolm.

They were quite some distance away and with the number of boats speeding by, neither of them could hear each other.

She saw them wave back rather wildly. She mistook their warning wave for agreement. Being impetuous she happily followed her new-found friends she had known for no more than a few moments.

On the Boat

Hailey had hardly got into the boat when she saw her friends rush toward her a bit too late. She was already on the boat as it began to pick up speed.

A few moments later, they break into a hearty laughter, as they watch her.

Hailey: She turns to the boatman and cheerfully asks him if she could pilot the boat?"

He moved aside with a smirk on his face and allows her to take the rudder. Hailey is unaware of his action when he presses a button.

They heard her scream. Filled with glee and fright, all at the same time especially when she tried to pilot the boat. They see her fall flat on her bottom inside the boat.

Everyone roared with laughter- those on the boat and her friends who kept watching. It seemed so hilarious.

Malcolm: "Come on let 's go and meet her." Dolton: "They usually come around the little island." He kept running along the shore.

Moments later the others followed suit. The women went panting unused to this exercise. Laughing and gasping for breath, they stopped.

All Eyes Sweep the Ocean

All eyes sweep the great expanse of water in front of them. But their laughter soon died when the last of the boats returned. Yes numerous boats landed but none in which Hailey was last seen.

They spoke to all the boatmen but none could throw light on this unfortunate affair.

One of the ladies: "Maybe, if you wait a little longer you will see the last of the boats. I thought I saw one, a distance away from us. They were going a bit too far away at an unusual speed. Everytime my family visits us, I come here and I have never ever seen, any of the speedboats that went such a great distance away- Strange!"

Another boatman joins in, "That's unusual our licence does not permit us to go any further than the stipulated, distance."

"Besides the fuel tank has a limited capacity!" Another cheerful driver added. He frowned. His expression showed he was perplexed.

And wait they did ….fifteen, twenty, forty minutes, an hour turned to a couple of hours with no sign of any boats coming to shore.

Their expressions portrayed tragedy. As time went on their anguish grew ... the only thing that mattered now was they needed to hear from her. Fear and apprehension of her friends grew more palpable.

Distraught
with Worry

Alice: "Why did we allow her to go by herself? This was her first visit here. We should have gone out of our way to make sure she was having a good time instead of being selfish and playing cards!"

She kept recriminating herself as she sobbed, imagining the worst.

Malcolm: "Stop that Alice! You are friends and there was no ulterior motive on both your parts. She decided to enjoy the waterfront and we the card game with no intention of hurting each other. This was just an innocent act which has turned out to be what it is. But we cannot jump to conclusions. There could be an explanation for this behaviour, so let's go home. There is a possibility we have a message on our landline as their cell could be out of range to contact us.

FRIDAY - DECEMBER 18TH.2004

At exactly 10:15 pm. they visit the police. The police goes through the formalities of asking them the following questions which infuriates them more than they imagine.

Cops: How well do you know your friend?
Alice: We correspond nearly every week.

Cops: "How long have you known her?
Alice: "For over three years;"

Cops: "Did they forcefully take her on the boat?"
Alice: "We do not think that was the case as we could see her laughing. She must have remembered the gentleman who had invited us for dessert, just yesterday at the restaurant. He is one of our friendly neighbours."

Cops: "Did you observe her on the boat with them? Was there any signs that she was pretending to be alright."
Alice: "I doubt it."

Cops: "When did you see her last, before her arrival here?"

Alice: "A couple of years ago.

Cops: "Does she like men a lot?"
Alice: "That's a rude question! I am going to ignore it."

Cops: "How long has she been married?"
Alice: "Fifteen years."

Cops: "Does she drink?"
Alice: "No, she's more for tea.

Cops: "Does she do drugs"
Alice: "She can't stand people smoking!"

Cops: "How well do you know her and can you trust her.?"
Alice: "We are like sisters.

Cops: "How did you meet her and in what circumstances?"
Alice: "This is ridiculous! We have been genuine friends and she is a very serious person. So please do not entertain ideas that are far from the reality. So if you do not mind, we will leave it to you to find her as soon as you can. Hailey is a close friend of mine and I know she is not capable of doing anyone any harm.

Cops: How old is she?
Alice: Thirty-five....But!

This seemed to take a turn for an intrusion, into her privacy.

Cops: We assure you our duty is to try to determine what had caused this disappearance.

But when they discovered her age they laughed.

Cops: "Don't worry she must be enjoying herself!"

One of them, added with a chuckle, "I think she is old enough to know what she is doing. Besides we can do nothing until she has been missing for more than forty- eight hours. We will get back to you when we have some information."

Cops: "Go back home and have a good rest. I am sure you will find your friend at your doorstep when you wake up."

DECEMBER 19ᵗᴴ. 2004

From then on every moment felt like an eternity. Once it was official it seemed all the more terrible. They went through her bags, trying to sort out if she held any hidden secrets of her life, but found nothing to explain her disappearance.

"I thought I saw Mr. Aziz in their company." commented Malcolm, "The few times I met him he seemed very friendly. I am sure he must have decided to take her along the coast. Let's go to the house they must have left a message for us on the answering machine."

Malcolm tried speaking in a reassuring voice which he didn't feel. He wrapped his arms around his wife trying to control the great fear that took hold of him.

The expression on Alice's face spelt fear. On their arrival home their first thing was to rush to the phone. To their great despair there was no message. They now feared the worst as the minutes went ticking by.

That night they gathered in Alice's living room waiting for a knock, a call.- anything, that might reassure them that the terrifying dread they felt was only the result, of their overactive imagination.

As time went by their anguish grew. Fear and apprehension of her friend's disappearance grew more palpable.

It is not possible that she left on her own volition. Some people vanish on a whim, but this didn't sound like that kind of a disappearance.

IN THE YACHT

*H*ailey: "Could I use your phone, my friends must be worried about me!"

Aziz: "I spoke to them moments ago. They are very happy that you are having a good time, so they did not think it was necessary to disturb you.

Hailey was having a whale of a time with her new- found friends. They were hilarious. All their little stories made her laugh to tears.

Hailey: "I haven't done, anything like this, in a long, long time! Thank you for your very kind invitation. I shall never forget this great experience! "And she never did.

All the screaming on the boat made her hoarse. She made as if to massage her throat. Aziz seeing this suggested, having a drink.

A thought crosses his mind. He says to himself, "Here's my grand opportunity!"

Hailey: "That would be very welcome. My throat is so sore!"

Jumma: "We always carry something with us, especially on a day like today!" She extended a flask. It was filled with cold kiwi juice!"

Hailey: "Thank you! Don't you want some too, she turned around offering it to the others. You must have some it's really refreshing and delicious!"

Sarita: "Yes, of course!" She stretches her hand out to Jumma. At that moment, the boat made a U-turn making Jumma drop the flask spilling everything. Hailey did not realize that she had intentionally done it.

Jumma: "Oh, no! I am very sorry." she said turning to Sarita as some of it splashed on her. Hailey in turn offered some of hers but they refused adding, "We just had some before this ride!" They answered in unison.

She did not realize that her drink had been laced with opium! She kept sipping at it. A few moments later she began to feel drowsy.

They arrived at one of the yachts that dotted the harbour. Aziz carried her into the yacht as she could hardly walk.

Her nearness excited him. He had an insatiable desire to touch her lips but he forced himself to quell the rising desire he felt, at least for the moment. So he kept his cool! He had to get her on board as soon as possible without drawing too much attention.

Feeling abashed although dizzy Hailey slurred

Hailey: "Do not worry just give me your arm." She slurred as she walked unsteadily. "I am just a wee bit dizzy. I can walk! It's the boat ride and I haven't slept much after the trip here."

She said in a groggy voice! A wan smile of gratitude spread on her face but was also filled with surprise wondering whether she was dreaming. She couldn't think with clarity.

These questions came slurring out of her mouth as she wobbled beside Aziz....

Where am I?

What am I doing here?

Am I really here in this strange environment? She was rather fuzzy-headed.

Moments later she had fallen into a deep slumber that lasted that whole night and nearly a day. It was six, in the evening, on Sunday.

DECEMBER 20ᵗʰ, 2004

*W*hen she woke up she felt strange as the bed seemed to rock a bit. She had hardly placed her feet, on the wooden floor when she heard a knock. Sarita came into the room.

Sarita: "Surprise! Surprise! Do you know you are in our yacht? Both Alice and Malcolm made arrangements with Aziz, to make sure you have a fantastic holiday. Since they are both working tomorrow they realized that this would be a great opportunity for us to show you around and make sure you have an unforgettable holiday."

Hailey: "Oh! She said drowsily. "That is very sweet of them. But they could have told me about it."

Jumma: "Aziz is very naughty. He kept everyone in the dark about his plans. For us it is a great pleasure to have you in our company for a couple of days."

Sarita:"Everyone here, have been waiting for you to wake up. We didn't want to disturb you. You will find everything that you need, here."

She sweetly said and walked away.

Hailey's surprise knew no bounds. She felt relaxed after the deep sleep, she knew not how long!

She realised that the room was richly decorated in pale pink with little magenta flowers, strewn around. No money was spared to make this a very comfortable place. She had never seen such luxury, soft silk sheets and cushions of Eider-down. A look of disbelief spread through her face as she continued to look around. She was amazed to see such luxurious, soft, silk carpets everywhere.

A furtive tenderness filled within her as she recalled that her dear friends had planned all this without saying a word to her.

A quick shower in this luxurious bath filled with strange piquant aromas seemed to stir her finest senses.

She wore the pale turquoise outfit with gold embroidery around the V-shaped neck that had been laid out for her. There were matching upturned pointed sandals. She pinned up her humid tresses high over her head as the hair- dryer couldn't be seen.

Little did she realise her luminous beauty. The setting sun, shone brightly, hitting her hair sending flashes of light as she went on deck, following their voices. She glowed with surprising sensuality but was completely unaware of it.

All eyes turn toward her filled with admiration that made her blush for a moment.

Aziz played the perfect gentleman and was up in a flash holding out his hand to steady her. He gave her hand a slight squeeze that sent a thrill through her body before he showed her to a deck-chair.

Nobody had showered her with such great attention. She felt flattered because her husband didn't seem to do any of these things for a long time. She was starving for affection. Aziz was a good reader of vulnerable women.

She was served a welcome cold mango juice. They said together: "You must be very hungry!"

Hailey: "Yes, I am. But if you don't mind I would like to talk to my friends before that."

"That was the first thing we did on arrival here." answered Aziz. "You had fallen asleep so we did not wish to disturb you."

"They were very pleased to know that you are having a good time. When I told them that you were sleeping they laughed."

Alice said, "Tell her to postpone her sleep for after her holiday!"

Not doubting him she didn't question his integrity.

She kept sipping her drink and decided to immerse herself in this delightful dream. She was naïve enough, not to realize that she was being twisted by manipulative powers far beyond her control.

They had some soft drinks, with pistachio, Iranian caviar and some other delectable snacks. The aroma and flavour played with her taste buds. This was followed by Jibeet - a desert made from date syrup and sesame seeds.

Sitting on deck she admired the ocean all around her. The view was breath-taking. Having lived in the mountains she had missed seeing the glow of twilight after that glorious sunset.

Every moment seemed to be a dream. During their meal there was some soft Arab music. She had never experienced such attention and service to detail.

Soon the lights from all the surrounding yachts came on. They kept shimmering on the water. The waves kept lapping against the yacht.

At about eight both Jumma and Sarita stood up.

GHE NÍGHG

Sarita:"Come on Hailey let's get ready for a promising night out. We have an invitation to the Burj Al Arab tonight. You must have heard about it! We shall be landing there, in one hour's time!"

Hailey: "I am very keen on visiting that hotel. Never dreamed, I would get that opportunity in such a short space of time."

Once they were in their cabins, Sarita held out a full length black cloak-like garment. She held it against, Hailey to check for the size. We call this garment the Abaya. It is made of silk. All women have to wear this when they go out. Although as you see we wear these beautiful clothes under it.

Today we will be attending the traditional dance.

Have you ever heard of the Ayyala? It's a traditional group dance of the United Arab Emirates. It is accompanied by traditional music, and a separate group of male and female are represented.

Yowalah is distinctive in both its music and dancing. Leather bagpipes, flute and drums are the traditional musical instrument played during the dance. It's now considered A Cultural Heritage by Unesco.

And of course we follow this with belly –dancing.

We will be dancing. There were three beautiful outfits of different colours purple, bottle green and pink hanging in the wardrobe.

"You will look gorgeous in this purple outfit!" Said Jumma. All the three outfits had embroidery made of gold threads, around the neck and around the hips.

All this seemed quite stimulating and exciting.

Hailey: "Did you say we? What do you mean? I don't have a clue. Now I hope you are not expecting me to join you in the dance."

She felt terribly embarrassed, rather shy, "Me, I don't know the ABC of how to do the Belly-dance. Yes, I would love to learn it! Would you teach me? "She asked in a soft voice.

"I just love dancing but this ah ! ah!"

She loved dancing and was a good dancer. "Yes, this is going to be a welcome experience for me. But not before I learn to do the dance. I am going to watch you!"

They were given strict instructions to do their best to change the appearance of Hailey.

Aziz had no intention of drawing too much attention and she would if they didn't do something to change this. He instructed the girls to make sure that she looked like one of them before they went to the hotel.

So they colour her hair as dark as theirs. They painted her eyes so that she did not look different from them. Dark make-up was applied to her face and her hands and feet were beautifully painted with henna.

"Do you mind if we colour your hair as Belly –dancers are all dark-haired!" asked Sarita.

They knew that Aziz was worried that she would draw too much of attention.

Hailey innocently agreed to all their suggestions feeling that they just wanted her to feel at home with them. She did not realize that Aziz had an agenda of his own. She wanted to please her friends so she would compensate them for their enormous kindness. Or maybe she was losing control over herself.

She thought it was hilarious when they decided to paint her eyes and made up her face with a darker shade. The end result, she didn't look very different from them, except for her eyes. They painted her lashes dark, to make her eyes as almond shaped as theirs. This added to the beauty of her eyes that shone startling blue.

Together they went up on deck where the men openly admired the women.

"You have changed, you look different. But it only adds to your incredible beauty!" said one of the men.

They were all wearing the black Bisht. Aziz was the first to complement Hailey. In a moment he was on his feet. He gave her his hand. He helped her with her long- flowing tunic, lest she tripped on it. They disembarked beside the hotel harbour.

They were shown to a very exclusive, luscious area. It was extravagantly furnished and clearly socially restricted. The three men and women got rid of their abaya and the bisht, and made themselves, very comfortable.

This surprised Hailey because she had been told that it was socially unacceptable. Women never did so publicly. Nor did the men!

The ambience was filled with a subtle, alluring quality. Here everything was exclusive.

The women then changed into their sexy belly- dancing clothes. They adorned themselves with long earrings and accessories to match and others that hung emphasising their hips.

"Aren't you looking forward to this moment?" asked Jumma.

"Yes," Hailey said. She was filled with ecstasy and maybe a wee bit uncomfortable, at the thought of getting on the floor doing something she had never ever done before in front of people she did not know very well.

"I prefer to watch you for a while before I dare to try it! I am looking forward to it.

Jumma:"You have to drink something before. This would help you loosen up a bit. You look a bit nervous.

She was dying of thirst, so she downed it in a moment. Little did she realise what she was doing. Besides she was nervous and excited at the same time. She was quite unaware of the great mistake as she was gullible and naïve to the point of negligence to trust everyone around her. What she did not realize was that all her drinks, was laced with opium.

They go in together to find the lights had been substituted for desert lanterns. It spreads a soft glow. The background was a simulation of tents. They lined the floor with exquisite silk carpets and cushions that felt soft to her naked feet. Their feet were painted with henna with the most beautiful paisley design, according to their plan. So were their hands too.

They served everyone some Aromatic Herbal tea.

They listened to some Arab music, followed by poetry and then the men began their traditional dance called the Ayyala.

Suddenly the lights were dimmed and her two friends Jumma and Sarita were seen as a soft spotlight focussed on them.

Hailey felt mesmerised as she watched them dance, mild at first but it soon turned erotic. She kept sipping her tea. Unaware that it was steeped with opium.

The drug and the atmosphere caused a dark passion boil under her subdued exterior. She did not realize but she was about to explode in a release of sexuality. She had been sipping her tea all that time.

She didn't need great persuasion, to get her to join them when they approached her. It was a kind of a sexual awakening. An excitement bursts within her far beyond her control.

The night seemed to promise exquisite joys she had never ever savoured before. She was on the floor as Sarita guided her.

At first she had difficulty trying to get her belly to move. But before long it seemed as if she had done it all her life. She was a fabulous dancer before! Her delicate honey- hued shoulders and the smooth, silky suppleness enhanced as she swayed to the rhythm of the music.

Aziz, his hunger to possess her, threatened to overpower the control he tried to exercise over himself.

After the dance, her friends conveniently disappear. She was left alone with Aziz.

He approached her and gently put his arms around her. Something over-powering took over her. Albeit she felt she wasn't her! A slight tremble went through her body. Much against her will she desperately wanted him but tried not to succumb to her feelings but it was beyond her control.

He took his time. He made her feel exclusive by persuading, cajoling in his soft deep voice.

He gradually undertakes her instruction in the art of sexual delight. He prepares her for the excitement of unleashing the carnal woman that was embedded within her – a temptation she couldn't resist.

The drug mixes with her hunger for sex. He walks her through a journey into the undercurrents of a world she had never known.

He genuinely cared for her so he took his time. He slowly explored her by beginning to slowly kiss her ears, her throat, her bare shoulders, her slender arms and fingers as he gently begins to strip her. Each time he gives her a gentle squeeze.

One garment at a time, as she just melts into his arms, his hands caressing, ran smoothly and gently all over her body – at first with soft feathers which made her tingle, revealing her milk-white silky skin, toned by the golden touch of the sun.

He kisses her breasts, licks at her nipples which were swollen, hard and he kisses her taut belly.

He seemed to fulfil something she wasn't getting in her marriage – her great hunger. She was completely lost, indulging in the carnal. She loses complete control and gets carried away- way beyond her realization about what had overcome her.

She is a pawn in a deadly power game created and stimulated by drugs she knew not. He uses all the words and phrases to soothe her conscience and makes her feel a valuable and beloved woman!"

Her body tingles with excitement with every delicate touch.

The great effect of opium kept creeping over her. She gets so drowsy that she soon falls into a deep slumber. Aziz lays her gently on the bed realising that he should not have had her drugged as much as they did. He didn't get to enjoy as much as he would have liked to. But this was through his, own fault, for having doubted his capacity to conquer her the way he would have liked to. He completely lost his head over her.

The next morning she was woken up by a tap on her door.

DECEMBER 21ˢᵗ. 2004

The next morning Sarita approaches Hailey's bedroom to find out how she was doing. She was a bit uncomfortable about the night before. A guilty feeling creeps through her body which lead to worrying about her friend. She was genuinely fond of Hailey. But she had no alternative but to follow instructions which she personally abhorred.

At first she tapped gently, but since there was no answer she nervously opens the door and knocks a book down as she couldn't see clearly in the dark as the shutters were down.

To Hailey's dilemma the sudden burst of light together with the feeling there was someone in the room she wakes up with a start, to discover she was in the nude all wrapped up in a soft pink silk sheet. She was filled with guilt.

Hailey realises that Sarita was in the room. "Just give me a moment, please."

Sarita leaves the room.

She jumps out of bed and grabs the night- dress that lay crumpled on the floor.

Numerous questions went through her head as she was getting dressed. She swayed a bit for a moment, feeling extremely tired. "You can now come in!"

Sarita had hardly entered only to see Hailey sway dizzily. Fortunately she was near enough to grab hold of her.

Despite her jealousy, she felt sorry for Hailey at the same time. Hailey had always been extremely good to her. She knew that Hailey had been drugged and its effect reflected on her face. She knew that Hailey wasn't the type to take drugs but she dared not explain anything to Hailey lest she has to face repercussions which she dreaded.

Sarita: "Just a moment. I think you should rest a bit. I am going to get you something to eat." She knew that Hailey hadn't eaten anything in hours.

Sarita decided to make her some food herself and to make sure it was something nourishing.

A few moments later she enters with a tray of sandwiches. They were made of mint with thin slices of anchovies and some tea. There was more milk than usual in the tea. She did not tell her that this would help clear up, the drugs that was in her body. She made sure it was real strong. She added extra honey to revive her energy. She did not order it from the kitchen instead she prepared it herself.

Now she did not trust anyone to help Hailey. It was clear to her what was happening and it pulled at her heart strings.

At first Hailey refused to have anything to eat but Sarita convinced her to first taste one. Hailey enjoyed the taste of mint, which she hadn't had for a long time. Sarita literally fed her. She was afraid she would drop the tray with the tea and sandwiches. Her hands tremble a bit. Despite her jealousy she felt very sorry for her. She knew that Hailey was there against her will. But she dared not say anything.

Hailey: "What's wrong with me? I feel rather strange though a bit better for the food though, thank you Sarita. You are very thoughtful and kind."

Hailey begins to wonder why she felt out of sorts, pretty dizzy, which had never ever happened to her before. She realizes she must have had sex with Aziz. This was clear. She was in the nude and this was unlike her. She could not remember anything. Her thoughts ran wild. It went here, there and everywhere. Thoughts floated through her brain. She felt that she must have enjoyed being with Aziz as her body seemed to crave to be with him.

Then her thoughts went to her friends, her husband. What would they think of her? In a way they were responsible for what had happened, for allowing her to wander about alone.

REGRETS

On second thoughts, "I was very selfish by not going with the flow. I should have been patient and tolerated playing cards with my friends. That could have been just a small sacrifice on my part for all that they were doing for me. They have gone out of their way to give me the very best. They were responsible for this visit to this awesome place for a holiday.

Her thoughts kept rampantly flowing towards her friends. She was filled with remorse and regretted her actions wishing she could do anything to undo her actions but this was no time for regrets but to look for solutions.

GHE NEW BEGINNING

That was the beginning of a new life for her. At first she indulges in the luxury that surrounds her. She experiences the novelty of having everything at her beck and call. Everything was new, exciting, unimaginable and way beyond her expectations!

Before long she began to realize that she was held captive. There were no chains, nor was she bound in any way physically. But the clearly unspoken rules were evident. They were not allowed out of the premises without a chaperon.

Outwardly they could shop freely and go wherever they pleased, to the most exclusive places. Everyone seemed to be very happy and more than comfortable with this environment.

But she realises there was clearly no escape for her. She now began to anxiously long for her freedom. Her companions, she discovered was used to this kind of life unlike her.

Hailey: "May I call my friends!"

They gave her a phone but when she connected she could hardly hear them, nor could they and so she hung up realizing it was futile.

There was nothing she could do and that something was seriously wrong with her.

Alice: "She is not herself! This is not the Hailey I know. Something is not all right. She sounds strange and we really do not know what they have done to her. But all the others began to think differently.

She has defrauded us. "Look at her calling us and then no explanation, no whereabouts. We barely heard a few words, come out of her mouth and that stuttering! What do we know about her really and truly? Don't you think she had to clarify the situation. I wonder if she realises how worried we all are. How dare she call us as if nothing has happened!"

Alice: "Do not rash-judge her! We just can't, jump to conclusions. I know her well. This is not the Hailey I know. My intuition tells me that she is not free to communicate with us. The call she made seems to have been manipulated. All we have to do is to pray for a miracle and that she finds a way out. The cops- well, is out of the question as this Aziz must be someone of distinction. He downplayed, his position, in a humble way that we got carried away. Or maybe that's part of his character. He has always been correct with us."

Another: "Maybe he really likes her. He did give us that impression at the restaurant, otherwise why would he send us that dessert."

Alice: "We weren't on such friendly terms! It was just a hello now and again when we crossed each other. Come to think of it, this is a rather an unusual situation."

Another: "They must have been following us to know that we had come to the beach. This couldn't be a co- incidence. We are neighbours and they must have seen us preparing for the beach- with all, the hamper. What followed just fell into place beautifully for Aziz!"

Hailey felt very disappointed, with the call she made. There was no way she could have a fluid conversation with her friends. Both their voices were breaking and far from clear. She could hardly exchange a few words with them. She felt trapped because she couldn't give them, any information, nor explanation about the all the time she has been spending away from them. Her life was not the same.

They did not realize that her life had taken a direction she knew not.

They were perplexed! The call she made only added fuel to the fire. They did not know exactly what was happening in her present life. As much as they wished to help her, they felt helpless as they had no inkling as to the what, where and how to help her.

With the exception of Alice most of her friends jumped to wrong conclusions.

"I am really disgusted with her behaviour. She must be carried away by all the luxury, they must surround her with. I overheard from one of the neighbours that Aziz is a Sheikh and a very rich one at that!"

Another friend: "Why has she put us through such great agony? She has the cheek of calling and then hardly saying anything- no explanation whatsoever! This is not the behaviour of a friend! To me she sounds like a slut!"

Alice: "How dare you! She is my friend! So please shut up. I am sorry but I feel you are being over-dramatic and imagining the worst of her. You are extremely rude. We really do not have an inkling of what she must be experiencing. I have heard some hair-raising stories. There's a possibility she is being treated very well but I doubt she has any freedom. From the call she made it was clear that she could hardly get through to us. In this modern world when phones are incredible, why do you think we could not have a decent conversation with her?

Alice poured out her outrage, filled with despair, not knowing how to approach this really unexplainable situation. She kept defending her friend.

Alice: "We have to give her the benefit of the doubt!"

One of them was filled with a great pity for Pierre who had since come to Dubai looking for his wife.

This was behaviour Alice least expected from her friend. But the doubt kept creeping within her which said that all was not as it seemed to be.

Hailey will never be heard of nor seen again. That's the impression they got.

HAILEY REALIZES
HER SITUATION

*I*t didn't take long before she begins to fill with despair, to discover that she was just a pawn in a power game where she finds herself attracted to the very man who holds her captive and keeps her as part of his Harem. So she was one of the many. She was treated like a queen. Aziz adored her.

She was in the lap of luxury. All that she desired, she just had to voice it and it was given. But her priced freedom had completely evaporated. She was not free to move around as and when she liked.

A great price to pay for the freedom she had longed for! All these past years, she felt like a caged bird. She wished to fly high and she did. In what way! Only to come crashing down to a very bitter reality where she didn't have the remotest possibility of escape for the much longed for freedom she had dreamed about. She was kept in a golden cage, all brilliant and beautiful but enshrouded.

She longed to be back, home, to her unassuming husband who not only provided for her but adored her. But routine took over and their love-life had a slow death as he took her for granted and did nothing but to fill her life with emptiness. But she had her freedom to go wherever she liked although he showed his displeasure.

All her hopes of escaping seemed futile. She was never alone.

But a small loop-hole existed.

She realized that Sarita was jealous of her. She used to be the favourite of Aziz but after Hailey's arrival on the scene, he hardly had any time for her.

She decided to watch Sarita carefully and went out of her way to be to be good to her. Often she would give her gifts which she knew made her very happy. It didn't take long before they became the thickest of thieves.

Fear of confiding in her soon disappeared.

This was something she wished to exploit, when she realized how desperate Sarita was to get Aziz back.

She got very close with Sarita. She got her to teach her to do the belly-dancing, so they had more time together.

Hailey decided that she had to find a way out of this ugly situation. She had to be very alert and agile for when and if the moment presented for her escape. She was careful what she ate. She didn't want to put on any weight. The Arabian food was very delicious, especially their sweets. She had a sweet tooth.

Hailey: "I have to observe my surroundings and everyone around me. But I have to keep this to myself until such time I am perfectly sure I can really trust someone.

She soon conquered all the style and grace of the professional belly-dancers but added the grace that Sarita adopted. This way should the opportunity arise they would not know the difference between them and maybe that would be the moment to escape. She wished to be part of the crowd and to play with time.

Each day her determination, of escaping one way or another became stronger. But she also realised that it was going to be extremely difficult but on rethinking she felt that nothing was impossible.

Every day she made sure to find some time to be alone with Sarita. They got so close that Sarita now got the message that Hailey would do anything for her. Sarita realised that Hailey was not really there to compete with her.

Now she realized that she had to be very careful and observant of her actions. She had to pretend when she was in the presence of Aziz. It was very difficult, but she knew how dangerous it could be, if he had the least suspicion of what she was planning to do.

So life continued, as if nothing had changed. But her wish to escape grew stronger each day. She dared not confide in anyone, nor change her routine or behaviour in any way, so she wouldn't draw attention.

Opportunity knocks at her door

Her opportunity came one night.

She could hear a muffled sound of someone crying.

She tiptoed out of her room to see Sarita leave Aziz room in tears.

She was tempted to approach her but decided to evade the issue at that moment.

The next day she discovered that Sarita's eyes were all puffed up, so she approached her.

Sarita: "You should not go around, looking like shit. Come on let me fix that pretty face for you."

Out came her toilet case.

Half an hour later, Sarita broke into a broad smile when she saw her face in the mirror.

Sarita: "Eh, how did you do that? Thank you." She gave Hailey a hug which is kind of unusual amongst them.

ᏛHE ᏒEVELAᏛIOꞄ

Hailey: "Now, can you tell why, you are so sad. Maybe I can help you?"

At first Sarita wondered whether she could confide in Hailey, but she remembered how she helped her a few moments ago and she very often gave her things she least expected.

Sarita: "Aziz wants me to go and spend some time with my family. But not before we celebrate the birthday of Prophet AL Mawlid Annabaoui. You see he has to see me dance on that day. He loves the way I do. I adore him. My life without him would kill me."

Hailey: "Well we have one week to prepare for that day. May I make a confession, but can I trust you? What if I told you, that, that could change. You may not have to leave this place. This is your home and has been for quite some time. I should be doing that, instead of you."

Sarita goes down her knees and hugs on to Hailey's feet! "Do you really mean that?"

Hailey: "Of course I mean every word I say!"

Sarita: "You must forgive me if I tell you something. I used to really and truly hate you. You stole Aziz from me. I used to be his great favourite. But after your arrival, he has no time for me."

Hailey: "I sort of felt that you didn't take to me. I also realized that you were terribly jealous of me. Do not worry, I understand you and I am going to make sure I change that for you."

Sarita: Amazed, "Do you really mean that? I was under the impression that you were crazy about Aziz. You seem to be so much in love with him. I have been very jealous of your relationship with him."

Hailey: "You are completely mistaken. I have been thinking of a way of escaping, for some time. I did not know who to trust and what to do. Do you know anyone who is trust-worthy? Can we confide in the girl who attends to you, or any of the waiters or waitresses at the restaurant? Who can we count on?"

Sarita breaks into a smile. "You surprise me greatly!"

Hailey: "Trust me, I will do all in my power to help you win your dear Aziz back and make your life happy again."

Sarita:"I will talk to Rani, the one who helps me. I give her a lot of presents and I know, she wasn't very happy with you being here. She knows all about me and how badly I was affected after your arrival here. She hates your guts. I will have to explain to her the real situation.

Aziz hardly ever talks to me. He calls me very rarely. And when he does I know he's just being polite.

I will talk to Rani. She has a brother who works in the hotel, too.

Hailey: "Is there any special occasion when we can divert their attention and find a way so I can escape, from here.

Sarita: "Yes the Sufi Zika could be our opportunity." Do you know anything about it?"

Hailey: "Isn't that the time, when the men dance in circles until they get into a trance?

I guess that is part of the celebration of the birthday of Prophet AL Mawlid Annabaou."

Sarita: "That will be the most suitable and only day when the men all disappear. We have a week to prepare for it, to minor detail. The smallest mistake will send both of us to the dungeons- the prisons. These are places were most people are terrified of. It is mostly a one way ticket to no return.

I will talk to Rani. I must be extremely careful.

It was well-known that most of the workers are terrified of repercussions. There is hardly any law for most of the migrants. They have no voice, nor, any help because most of the workers are terrified of reprisals. They get thrown into prison with no questions asked and treated in the most degrading manner. They literally belong to the company that employs them…meaning they have no option to change companies as and when they wished. Their passports were held by the company.

Hailey: "Just a moment."

Sarita: "Aziz told me a few days ago that he wanted to see you do the Belly- dance. He added that I could relax a bit. He did not realize how very sad and disappointed I felt when he said that to me." She let out a deep sigh and looked very sad.

Hailey interrupts: "I just got an idea. Since we have been practising together a lot and I really can see no difference between the two of us, why can't we switch places for the belly-dancing?"

Sarita: "But your eyes will give you away!"

Hailey: "Isn't there a way of getting contact lens? I know that today you can get them in a couple of colours. You can wear blue ones and I can wear black. Let's check it out in one of the places that we visit at the Souk.

Sarita: Wonderful! The lights are usually dimmed to add to the sexuality, during the dance. So it is not easy to see the difference in the soft lights."

Hailey: Besides don't we have to wear veils over our faces. I have seen it done often or is it a common practise. This will also help hide the differences between us.

Sarita: Well that's what we do. We wear the veils, over our face but our eyes are uncovered. The veil, is amazing, an added touch of sexuality that emphasises the eyes so that's one of the reasons why they are painted beautifully.

The next day Sarita convinces Jumma to go on a shopping spree. So the three of them woke up all excited with plans to check on what was new again in the market. This was a pastime they really enjoyed. They only shopped in exclusive, brand name shops. No money was spared. They always got the best.

tHE SHOPPING SPREE

Once they were at the souk, Sarita and Hailey had planned to be careful. According to their plans Sarita would have to find a way to distract Jumma while Hailey was looking for contact lenses.

Her excuse, should she be discovered was that she would like to look like them and not feel different. But the blue contacts, was for Sarita.

ᏖHE CONᏖACᏖ

*H*ailey approaches the salesman smiling.

The Salesman observes Hailey straying towards the section for contact lens. This surprises him. He observes her examining them in detail, especially the blue lens. He goes towards her.

Wearing a broad smile he approaches her. He quite liked her. Her taking ways attracted most people. "What can I do for you? I was wondering whether you really want something from this department or maybe you are a bit lost."

Hailey: "I was looking for coloured lens. I am a wee bit tired of looking different."

Salesman: "What colour are you looking for?"

Hailey: "Black would be great!"

He shows her and explains the differences between them- quality-wise. She chooses one, pays for it and moves away.

She had hardly moved a couple of paces when she turns around. A sudden thought creeps into her brain. She walks toward the Salesman.

Salesman: "Did you forget something or have you repented for having bought the lens?"

Hailey: "On second thoughts I think it will be neat if I can make my friends look like me and have the same colour eyes as I do. Don't you think that's a great idea?"

The salesman gives a knowing smile. He was very not only intuitive but very observant. He had been observing Hailey. He noticed as time went on that now and again he captured fleeting moments of sadness reflect on her face. So when she asked for lens he suspected that she had an ulterior motive. He knew she would do no harm to anybody. He genuinely liked her. At that moment he decided that if she ever needed any help from him, he would do all he could.

Hailey: "It would be an exciting present if I give my friends this. They always envy my blue eyes. Do you see those friends of mine I would like to buy each of them blue contact lens. But I would like it to be a surprise so I don't want them to know anything about my buying both the colours. So please don't mention anything to them.

Salesman: "That's very thoughtful of you. No problem. I'll make sure they do not see it. I shall pack it up separately in such a way it would not be seen by them. Besides they seem to be very busy with other things. He realised that Hailey needed help. But he was also sure that she would do no harm to anyone. He had taken a liking to her. Hailey made everyone feel special.

Hailey was a very sweet person. Most of the women in her status carried an air of great arrogance which she lacked. She always wore a smile and was always gracious and appreciative. She didn't consider it their obligation to deal with clients with deference.

Hailey realised that time was flying by and each day just made things worse for her in the sense she felt she couldn't handle this situation. She had a few days left. A sudden thought struck her.

"Why can't I use the salesman. I am aware that he does have a soft corner for me. He always goes out of his way to show me, the newest and the best clothes that come into the market."

That day she reaches the decision of asking for his help.

PREMEDITATED SHOPPING SPREE

*H*ailey: "I forgot that I should buy some eye- drops, should they ask me why I was at your shop."

Salesman: "You are a very smart lady. Good for you. I shall get the very best for you. It is safe to use it whenever wish, especially when you go to the beach. It will protect your eyes from dust and wind."

Out of the corner of her eyes Hailey spotted Aziz coming her way. She was quick-witted. On the spur of the moment she realises that it would be a great excuse to get him a present. She turns around to the salesman.

Hailey: "I would also like to buy a pair of sunglasses. This could be a present for Aziz. Show me the best and the latest but a unique one that could suit him."

She chooses an exclusive pair of sun-glasses by Versage. This could be another excuse for the packet she had in the bag. She pays and is about to leave that department when she Aziz comes toward her from around the corner. There was nowhere to escape. She quickly approaches the salesman.

Hailey: "Please don't tell anyone about my lens. It is going to be a surprise."

He readily agreed. Hailey was one of his favourite customers. She always bought the best, which meant added revenue for the company.

Hailey realises that she now has him, as accomplice. She could count on him, should she find herself in jeopardy.

Sarita used their shopping spree to give Rani a day off.

Aziz: "Eh! What are my pretty ladies doing here?"

Hailey: "Well don't think that we are always thinking of ourselves when we go shopping. I found you something that suits you beautifully. May I?" She hands him the packet. It was a pair which was very fashionable among men.

The alert salesman knew the taste of most men, just like himself. So when Aziz opened the packed he broke into a smile. "It's so like you to be ever thoughtful. You have great taste. You didn't really have to do this, but coming from you makes me feel very special. "Thank you!"

Hailey: "This was supposed to be a surprise for you but now that you are here, I had this something to enhance your handsome face."

Aziz looks a bit flushed as he was caught unawares. His face was filled with pride to see someone show how much they cared for him publicly.

"I never expected you to come out with something for me. I should be the one buying you something!"

The shopping spree had been well planned by Hailey. It was a great success. Everything fell well into her plans. She needed the lens and got it problem free. She also wanted to give Rani and her brother some time together.

RANI'S PRIORITY

Rani grabbed this opportunity to spend more time with the family also to discuss how they could help both Sarita and Hailey. Sarita was their priority. Sarita gave her an envelope with money, which she did now and again because she knew that she had a family to maintain. This time Hailey helped by adding a sumptuous amount.

THE PLOT

Rani: "Anand, there is something I would like to talk to you about."

Anand, "You look so serious so this must be something very important. You scare me with that expression on your face."

Before she approached the subject she handed him the envelope. On opening it, his first reaction was.

Anand: "My dear sister you didn't steal this by any chance. His eyes open wide, filled with fear, when he sees the quantity of money. Where did you get this? Did you steal this?"

Rani: "Are you crazy? Sarita gave me this money."

His eyes open wider with enormous surprise which turned to fear.

Anand: "Why would she give you so much?"

Rani: "I don't know what you would think about this. Maybe she needs some help."

Anand: "I don't know what it is, but just the sound of it, terrifies me. I hope it is not going to be dangerous."

Rani: "You know Hailey, the newcomer, well I suspect she wants to go back home and doesn't know how to go about it. She is terrified of talking to anyone about it. Do you think we could help her? This will help Sarita a great deal. You know how badly Aziz has been treating her since the arrival of the newcomer. Besides, Hailey has given Sarita money to hand it to me. She would like to help our parents.

Anand: "Forget about it! This is very dangerous and nearly impossible. Get all that rubbish, my dear sister out of your head!"

Rani: "Now relax brother! She desperately wishes to escape. Why can't we help by using the day of the Sufi Zika, which is an auspicious day. You must know that this is an unusual opportunity for all of us, when all the men are very busy."

Anand, "That's a very appropriate day. But how does she get out of here?"

Rani, "Well, that's when you could come into the picture."

Her eyes fill with tears. She was very attached to Sarita. With her palms together she pleads, "Don't you realise how much Sarita has been suffering since the arrival of Hailey. To make matters worse now he wants her to leave the house and spend some time with her parents. In other words he wants to get rid of her."

Anand: Yes most of us have noticed the great change after her arrival here. Aziz is madly in love with Hailey. She is not a bad person. Everyone adores her. She is really very popular. I am not surprised at that. She is far from presumptuous. She treats everyone kindly. Her taking ways have captured numerous admirers, here. She is not only outstanding in beauty but her behaviour is amazing. All the more we have to be extremely careful. Nobody should get an inkling of our plans."

Rani: "If you think we could help I'll tell Sarita, that maybe she could suggest that now is the best time to escape if Hailey is not happy here. There are moments when she looks lost and often a little sad. We have a week. Do you think she could escape dressed as a man, so she won't draw too much of attention while all the men are running towards joining in the Sufi Zika?"

Anand, "Are you really sure that Hailey wants to go away? Well, the Thobe and head gear is a must in such a situation if she wants to move around unrecognised. It is the best way to go unnoticed. During this specific period everyone is too busy to pay attention to anyone who looks no different from them. But we have to be careful of the girl who takes care of her. You know how everyone is terrified of breaking the rules her."

Rani, "Is there a possibility of you using the van you work with. Maybe you could use the van for the laundry. An added bonus is that she will be wearing, rather there is a possibility that she wears black contact lens so she will not draw too much of attention. I overheard Sarita and her discussing about the lens. Should she cut her hair short hair it could be hidden under the head gear.

Anand, "My dear sister you have been working that brain of yours overtime. You must really want Hailey out of here or adore Sarita."

Rani, "What do you think? And can I count on you before I reveal all my ideas to Sarita?"

Rani is carried away with her suppositions. "During this week she could pack some of her clothes each day, so she will not be seen taking anything except rushing out as if she was going for the Zika. Once she is in the lift you should be there. You go directly to the basement, to the laundry room. She could either sit next to you or hide amongst the clothes. Whatever you think is safe."

Anand, "Before we continue with all these plans make sure she really wishes to leave. I know how very worried you are about protecting Sarita.

The next day Rani talks to Sarita about all that she had discussed with her brother.

Rani speaks, "I have a feeling that now is the time for Hailey to leave. I have observed her and noticed that she isn't all that happy she pretends to be. I have discussed this with Anand and he has agreed to help her leave."

Rani speaks to Sarita, "At the dance I will take your place and you can dress just like Hailey. Since the lights are dim. They will not notice the difference especially with the preparation of going to the Sufi Zika. Then she spills out all that she had discussed with her brother. Although Sarita was taken aback, she was pleased with the details."

Sarita, "How thoughtful of you to have gone to such great extend to find a solution to my problems. I can never thank you enough, although, we do not know if this is going to work but it sounds very plausible.

She plans to approach Hailey when she had a quiet moment when she and Hailey were alone.

A couple of days later she had the opportunity to do so. This was usually a time when everyone had a nap. She knew that most often Hailey sat in the garden in a quiet corner with a book. That's when she reveals, all that Rani had discussed with her. At first Hailey was shocked at the idea but very pleased, at the same time. She realises that the plans were well calculated and seemed feasible to her.

Sarita: "Hailey you can play sick with Jumma. So she will mention that to Aziz that you weren't feeling well and that I will be taking your place in the dance. That would be more feasible than pretending to be another.

Hailey: "No, we should not tell anyone, anything. Jumma should be in the dark about all our plans. I have the lens I picked up at the shop. So you will wear blue lens. I would use that moment when you begin to dance, to escape.

Sarita: "Well, that is a great idea!"

Hailey, "You will have to make sure you wear blue lens and wear my clothes. He usually sends me the clothes for the occasion. We have to be fast."

Sarita, "But we also have to remember that you are somewhere, where nobody can trace you. Aziz has numerous friends in the right places.

Hailey: "We could take advantage of both situations as they are both on the same day. We have one week. Do you trust your friends? I have to get a message to Alice.

Sarita, "That's the first place they will check. It's better they know nothing until you are, safely home.

Hailey, "How do I leave from here?"

Sarita: What we need is a thobe, a hijab and a turban for you to wear. In the rush, for the men to join the Sufi Zika they may not notice your escape if you dress like one of them.

Hailey: "The clothes- that's one thing but the escape as such is not going to be easy. We will have to meet with Anand and Rani."

Hailey, "What worries me is that I am most of the time being watched. The best time for me to escape would have to be during the Belly-dancing. We have to make sure that nobody, and nobody should have an idea, about what we propose to do."

Sarita: We have completely forgotten Nora who looks after you. She is very fond of you but can we trust her. You should try and get as many details about her family. What do you know about her background? Most of the people who work here have their families dependent on them. None of them would risk their lives to be either thrown in jail or to end up being jobless.

Hailey, "The first thing they would do is to go after her. So I do not think that's a great solution. I recall what she had discussed with me some time ago, when she saw me crying one day."

Nora: "Mam have you ever thought of leaving this place?" Yes I can see Aziz is crazy about you but you never know how long this will last. He used to adore Sarita but once he laid eyes on you, he discards her. What if he sees another, women, younger and more beautiful? The same could happen to you, too.

This conversation took place a month before.

It suddenly dawned on Hailey the possibility of using Nora, as an accomplice, too. Hailey had loads of jewellery. Most of it was of pure gold. This could fetch a great deal of money. Money was not the major problem, at this moment. She would readily share it with Nora. She could live a very comfortable life in her country with this added money and wouldn't have to work here any, more.

CHANGE OF PLANS

*H*ailey decides to say nothing at that moment but she recalled all that they had discussed about her escape with Sarita.

She realises that it seems as if each time the ring was growing bigger. There's Rani, Anand, Sarita, and now Nora, that's getting too many people involved. Under torture any one of them could confess so why should I have all these people involved.

The next day she tells Sarita that she had changed her mind about leaving. Sarita was awfully disappointed.

Hailey: "I do not want you to get involved in such a dangerous situation."

Sarita was terribly disappointed. "I realise that his could be a problem, for everyone. After all is said and done, you are very comfortable here. Do not worry about me. It will just be a week away. I know Aziz will not let me down. We are very close although he appreciates you more than I. But we are good friends and I would not like you to have any problems. So let us leave it as is."

Hailey: "So Sarita, I hope you don't mind but it is better for everyone I stay and keep everyone out of trouble."

But that was far from what she was thinking. As each day dawned she became more determined to leave one way or another. She realises that it was very dangerous to depend on so many people. Under duress anybody could confess. Besides she thought it pointless and unnecessary to involve her best friend Sarita

Sarita was not too pleased with this, but she knew that Hailey was taking her into consideration. It was the best for everyone. She knew that Hailey cared for her very much.

A BRAIN WAVE

ailey soon began to look for excuses to go shopping. Jumma and Sarita loved shopping too. This posed no problem for her. She decided to visit this boutique. Arjun made sure his shop was always one step above the others. Arjun was the name of the salesman. She later discovered that he was also the owner.

She gets a brain-wave. She recalls the moment when he sold her the lens. He seemed like someone who would not tell on her. She recalls when she asked him not to mention, to the others when she bought the lens and he didn't. He could easily have done so. He owed her nothing.

He always seemed very pleased to see her. This time she slipped him a note, while he handed her a piece of clothing she wanted to buy.

Hailey, "My husband is very ill. I am very anxious to go home. But as you must already know they will not allow me to go. I am held here against my wishes. They give me the best but I desperately wish to go back home. This is not my home. I don't belong here. CAN, YOU HELP ME!"

He made as if he was putting by the clothes, while he was attending another customer. He read her message.

Arjun: "Madam your wish is granted I found something you really like!" He emphasized the words … your wish is granted.

They left the shop all excited with the new clothes they had bought. Once arriving at their place Hailey says, "I must have left my dress on the counter, because I don't have it with me."

FORGOTTEN PACKET

A knock on the door, breaks the silence. Hailey opens the door.

Salesman says loudly, "You had forgotten your dress in the shop!"

He hands her the packet and leaves immediately. She thanks him profusely. But he didn't hang around.

Salesman: "I am in a hurry!"

He didn't want to draw any attention. It seemed like a curtsy call.

She quickly took the bag into her room. The moment she was alone she opened the bag and amidst her silk outfit there was a small note. She read it, tore it to pieces after memorising it and flushed it down the toilet without much ado. Amidst her dress she was given a safety belt, so she could carry her most important jewellery.

Hailey had decided to follow part of the plan she made earlier with Sarita. But of course she didn't mention that to her.

She decided to wear the Thobe, the hijab and a turban. Under those clothes she could wear the safety belt. Here she could carry her jewellery and her money.

This way she would not draw too much attention. She made sure that Nora was at the dance. This time she lazed Nora's drink, so that she would be a bit high and wouldn't realize the change between her and Sarita.

THE MESSAGE

The message she had received from Arjun was explicit.

"At exactly 4p.m when all the women had gone down to the dance floor, you will accompany them but as soon as you have finished, you have exactly half an hour to get into the thobe, the hijab and wear the turban. Most of guests would have left after the Belly dancer. The men would all leave immediately after the program, for the Sufi Zika."

CHANGE OF PLANS

*H*ailey realises there may not be enough time for her escape. So she decides not to join the belly dancers.

Hailey prepares some make –up so she looks really ill. Besides she pinches her cheeks really hard so it turns completely red.

The moment Sarita enters the bedroom, she sees the feverish appearance of her friend. She had lost her usual lustre. A perplexed look flashes across her face when she sees Hailey in bed.

Sarita: "You don't look well, is everything alright. Looking at you tells me you should see the doctor!" When she approaches Hailey stops her.

Hailey: "You should be down with the others. I have been feeling nauseous and puking for the past couple of hours, so I decided to stay in bed. So go on and enjoy yourselves, everyone must be waiting for you. You better hurry. I will be fine with this tea, which I just ordered. This usually settles my stomach. By the time you come back I shall be fine."

Sarita: "Now we will miss you at the dance. Everyone is going to be very disappointed."

Hailey: "Now I think, you should take my place. You can wear these, blue lens so nobody will notice the difference. Now please wear these clothes Aziz brought especially for this occasion. I do not wish to worry him. I better stay in bed. I do not wish to mess up the place."

She waited for Sarita to leave, but decided to wait a couple of minutes more just in case she comes back or if Jumma wishes to visit. Fortunately she stayed because unexpectedly Aziz walks in.

Aziz: "I just met Sarita and she mentioned that you were indisposed so I decided to visit you. Yes you do look ill. You better stay in bed I will see you after the Sufi Zika. It will give you enough time to relax!"

Hailey hoped that Sarita would not wear the blue lens, if that happens Aziz would realize that that was rather fishy. Hope Sarita realises after meeting Aziz she would not have to wear her clothes nor the lens.

With that he left her after giving her a peck on her cheeks. She lay trembling for a moment. She realises that she had just escaped by the skin of her teeth. Had he come ten minutes later he could have caught in the act of escaping. She was very fortunate.

About to jump out of bed, she had her legs out of the bed, when she heard another tap and Jumma walked in. In went her feet once again under the coverlet.

Jumma: "Just came to say get better! Aziz mentioned that you were ill. I do not wish to disturb you, go back to sleep." With that she left.

Hailey realises that Sarita shouldn't be wearing her clothes, nor wear the blue lens. She tells Jumma to ask Sarita not to look for Aziz. He just came by to see me. She hoped Saria would get the message. Enjoy the dance. I am sorry to miss such exciting moments."

ᏮHE PLAN

Arjun enters the hotel. He approaches the busy receptionist.

Arjun: "Hello, Suresh how are you today?" he approaches the receptionist, all smiles. They knew each other very well. Arjun usually visited the hotel now and again. He was well-known and appreciated by everyone there.

Suresh, "Very busy, more than I can chew! He says without lifting his head from the desk.

Everyone is busy running around making sure they will not be late for the Sufi Zika."

Arjun: "The ladies were so excited this morning. They had done quite a lot of shopping that one of them dropped one of their packets. I am sorry I couldn't come earlier!"

Suresh, "You will do me a great favour by handing it to them directly, and thank you. Well knowing them as well as I do they must be occupied with today's extraordinary show. It's a pity I can't attend the program. Belly-dancing is thrilling it brings out the outstanding beauty of the dancers. But today I was told that Hailey is participating too. I would have loved to attend it.

Arjun: "I better get going!"

He didn't wish to waste a minute. Time was the essence. The faster he was out the better.

He had instructed Hailey to walk calmly to the waiting limo that was at the door of the hotel, while he distracts the receptionist. Arjun although he was well- known, did not want to take any chances.

Hailey walks calmly down the hall. She made sure the heels she wore wouldn't make the slightest of noise especially on the plush carpets. She was lithe and agile and made it to the limo in a fleeting moment.

She slips into the open limo which had smoked glass windows. Arjun joins her, ten minutes later. His brother, the driver takes off as fast as possible. Now this being a day when everyone was in a hurry, their speeding through the streets did not draw too much of attention. They sped by without a problem.

Once they are in the car, he began to explain his plans.

Arjun: "I am taking you home to my wife. She will do all that is necessary to avoid drawing too much of attention to you. There is a hairdresser waiting for you. They will strip your hair of all, the dark colour and once again you are going to be your true self- the blonde beauty." He added with a smile. You will also get back into your European clothing."

His wife hands her two bags with clothes that befitted her standing. They seem to have thought about everything. Fortunately

Aziz had never taken her passport which is typical in the country. Women did not usually travel alone.

He handed her a ticket direct to Spain.

He handed a fake telegram which said she had to be home for the funeral of one of her family members.

She wore a black raw-silk suit.

Arjun drove her to the airport. He drops her near the Turkish Airlines gate. He unloads her bags, puts them on the trolley and wishes her goodbye.

INSIDE THE AIRPORT

There were very few Customs Officers, that day at the airport. It was a holiday in the Muslim world. Hailey stiffened and turns white, when she saw one walk toward her. She keeps cool. She pretends not to see him and tries to walk past him. But he approaches her.

Custom's Officer: "Hello there!"

He was all smiles! Her fear evaporates and is replaced with a warm feeling when she hears him speak. "It is good to see you again!" She gives out a deep breath. He was not going to get her into trouble.

"Did you enjoy the Cultural Show? Of course without you artists it couldn't be a great success. Thank you, for your participation. We look forward to seeing you again."

She thanks him profusely. "The pleasure was mine. Amazing hospitality I shall never forget."

He stamps her passport.

She gives a deep sigh of relief. "In a couple of hours I shall be back in my own turf!" Tears of joy fill her eyes. "It will not be long before I shall be boarding my flight to freedom."

She coolly walks past gates until she reaches gate 45. She paralyses when she sees another officer. Hands outstretched he approaches her smiling. She relaxes, once again.

"So now you are on your way back home, don't forget to come back, next year! It has been our pleasure, to have had you amongst us."

Thanking him profusely, she moves on, feeling more relaxed.

She finds a comfortable seat and closes her eyes. She impatiently waited to board her flight. All the tension of the last few days began to take its toll. She opens her phone and decides to spend some time on meditation, to get rid of everything negative that she had built up within.

She had nearly dozed off, when she heard the announcement that woke her up with a start: "In fifteen minutes we will begin boarding. Her excitement grew: "At last I shall be free and back home again."

While she was standing in the queue, another announcement was made. Due to weather conditions the flight to Istanbul has been delayed until further notice.

Her pulse dropped. Hailey knew she had no time to play with. This upset her completely. Her reflexive reaction was to pick up her hand bags and make a move as fast as she could, not knowing what direction to take. All she knew was, she couldn't stay there a moment. She stumbles out, as she rushes past the security guard hoping to pick up the first cab and get out of the airport.

intuitive action

*J*ust as Anand was about, to drive away, a sudden thought, held him back. He thought to himself. "I am not in a hurry I might as well wait here just in case she needs something she might have forgotten."

He parks his car in the airport parking and decides to walk along the area where he had dropped her.

Moments later he not only over heard the announcement but he sees this message flash on the screen - All out-going flights to Turkey have been delayed due to a snow storm.

Hailey was flying Turkish Airlines. It was impossible to leave Istanbul. Most of the airports in Europe are closed until further notice. There was a snowstorm and all the airports were closed to traffic due to the difficulty on the snow-covered runways.

Arjun had to think fast. "I had booked her on the first flight that was leaving Dubai but now we have to have a change of plans!"

He could not enter the airport. All he could do is hope that she will not stay inside and come out as soon as possible. He kept walking up and down when suddenly...

Hailey is surprised but very, very happy. "Arjun! Arjun! I am here, once again." He hears her shout.

"Stay where you are, I am going to pick up my car! Don't worry, I heard the announcement. I will take you home nobody will suspect you of being with us."

Hailey: "What happens to my bags that I had checked in?"

Arjun, "That's the least of your problems right now. Frankly speaking they were checked directly to Spain and that's where you can pick them up. It will be safe there. What we do have to worry is about our next move."

Hailey: "As regards going to your home is a No...no....not now! I feel the best bet is to go straight to the Embassy. This will keep you out of all these problems and I feel more secure as I will have all the protection I now need. I sincerely appreciate all that you and your amazing wife have done for me."

Hailey did not wish to offend him. She realised that he was going out of his way to do all within his capacity to help her.

Hailey: "You must realise that too many people work for you and they all know me and we never know how the scene could change. I have to think of the best way out of this problem and protect you, too."

Hailey realises that she was in a fix. Thoughts one after the other kept going through her mind. I think I should call my friend and let her know what's happening…then not my friend Alice…. No …No… Noo! I don't want her to be involved with my problems.

Arjun realises that Aziz would not take too easily to losing her. He was crazy about her and would leave no stones unturned to get her back. No one knows what his re-action would be.

Hailey knew Aziz was completely carried away with her. He would do all in his power to find her. He would pull all the strings wherever possible, within his reach. So let us keep to my going to the Embassy."

Arjun: "Call the Embassy to warn them of your arrival there. I think that's the best thing to do, right now."

Hailey: "No, any calls from me could be traced. Please take me to the Embassy, without further ado."

So once again she is in his car en-route to the embassy.

They were just a few metres from the Embassy when suddenly out of nowhere a car comes crashing into them.

Fortunately Hailey had a change of heart, just half an hour before had decided that it was the right thing to call the Embassy.

So while Arjun was driving she dials the Embassy.

"I am Hailey Anderson from Spain. I do not know if I have been reported missing. I was kidnapped and have just escaping hoping to catch a flight home. But that was an impossible dream as all the flights have been cancelled and I am now en-route to the Embassy. Please, pleeese meet me at the entrance. She gave them details of the car Arjun was driving.

This sudden, intuitive call really reached the Embassy at the most appropriate time.

AFTER THE
BELLY DANCE

Sarita fortunately decided at the last minute not to take the place of Hailey, nor wear her exclusive, clothes that Aziz had bought especially for her.

Moments before the dance, Aziz approached her. "Make sure you see that Hailey is very well as soon as the dance is over. If there is any problem please let me know as soon as possible. I will make sure a doctor visits her right now!"

Jumma; "I just crossed Aziz. He was coming out of Hailey's room, so he knows that she is not very well. Hope the rest will do her good. She was terribly disappointed not to take part in the Belly-dancing.

Nora is still a bit groggy from the stiff drink Hailey had prepared for her. How is Hailey?"

Sarita: "I saw Hailey rushing up to her room. She looked awful. She said that she felt nauseous. Let's go and see how she is, now."

Nora, "That's right, she was retching out when I left her. When I offered to stay with her she refused. She insisted that she wanted me to leave her alone and that she needed to go to bed."

Hailey: "Nora you better go and enjoy the belly dancing. You are not going to solve any problems by staying beside me rather you will be disturbing me. I want to go to bed and not be disturbed." These were the ords Nora recalled.

mistake uncovered

Jumma and Sarita knocked gently on the door but since it was open they burst into her room. But when they see her all covered up, they tiptoed out lest they would disturb her much needed sleep.

What they did not realize was Hailey made it seem as if she was in bed. She fluffed up the quilts and she packed the cushions to seem as if someone was in bed, before she left. This did the trick. This also gave her more time for her escape.

GHE SUFÍ ZÍKA

I
t didn't take long before the men began rushing from all directions.
They began going round and round in circles, while others just
went on their knees and kept swaying and spinning forward and
backward. They kept at it until it seemed they were in a trance.

HAILEY IS MISSING

wo hours went by so Nora decided to check on Hailey once again. She opens the door softly. She quietly approaches the bed.

She lays the tea and cookies she carries, on the bedside table.

Terrified she could not hear Hailey breathing. Very slowly she lifts up the silk sheets and jumps with a start. Low and behold, she wasn't there! So she ran to the toilet. The door was locked from the inside. "Hailey! Hailey! Are you alright?"

She kept tapping, fearing the worst, as no answer came from Hailey. She rushed to Sarita's room. Soon Sarita and Jumma went to Hailey's room but no answer. So they approached the receptionist who sent someone to open the door. "Did Hailey call for help? Maybe someone took her to the hospital?"

The moment the door was opened they were astounded. At first, they gave a deep sigh of relief that she wasn't dead. They then burst out into nervous laughter.

"Can't you understand this means she is alive. We were under the impression that we could find her dead inside." They turn to the receptionist who had a worried look on her face.

Sarita and Nora exchanged knowing glances. They were sure she had left and were grateful to God. But this feeling soon evaporated when they realized they will be all taken to task, through no fault of theirs.

Nora: "Sarita you look upset. You don't have anything to worry about. You are not responsible for this situation. Fortunately everyone, were under the impression she was ill. All of us saw how very ill, she looked.

Sarita: "I remember the worried look on Aziz face. He managed to see her at the right time, just before he left. He asked me to check on Hailey, immediately after the dance. But Sarita felt very guilty all the same, about the whole situation.

Jumma, "What are we going to say to Aziz? Maybe she has been kidnapped by someone. When did you last see her Sarita?"

Sarita: "Just like you before the Belly-dance!"

Just then they see a note pinned on to the pillow.

"I am very sorry to put all of you through this dilemma. I had to leave the country on such a short notice. My friends had been desperately looking for me. With great difficulty they discovered where I was and came to pick me up so that I could attend the funeral of one of the members of my family.

There was no way, nor time for me to contact anyone.

Strange as it may seem I was really ill as you all know. I must have intuitively felt that something was wrong in my home front.

Thank you all for the most enjoyable and unforgettable, period of my life I spent with each of you especially Aziz- to whom I owe a great deal.

A CHANGE OF PLANS

Hailey had been determined to find a way to escape the dance. She managed to convince not only Sarita that she was feeling very ill. Sarita didn't doubt it when she saw her puke a number of times.

One of Hailey's suggestion had been to Sarita, to take her place, in the dance. She did not wish to upset Aziz. That was to be the moment when they could distract everyone by getting her to wearing the blue lens. But all that was unnecessary after she played sick.

The day before, she bought some beautiful jewellery for both Sarita and Rani. This did not surprise them. They were used to receiving gifts from her, but what they did not realize was, that that was a parting gift.

Sarita recalls her conversation with Hailey just before the dance. Fortunately this didn't take place as she met Aziz before and realised all that was futile.

THE ACCIDENT

A car came out of nowhere, just as Arjun was getting out of the airport area. He slams on the brakes to avoid the accident, when another car comes ramming into him. He swings to his right but the other, a young driver decides to do the same and wam..bang.. bang…the other cars from behind come crashing onto them.

The initial impact causes their car to change direction and pushes it right into the path of another that followed into other oncoming traffic causing the bizarre, multiple impact with numerous drivers all rushing to be at the Sufi Zika.

ᏲHE CHAOS

The efficiency of the City Officials was outstanding. In the matter of minutes, Emergency flashing lights and the sharp sound of the yelp siren - the police shrill distinct ee-o—ee—oo – column of emergency vehicles, the wail and the howl waaaaallhhhhhh of fire protection engines and power unit disengagement specialists all arrive simultaneously.

Out comes, chocks and the jaws- of- life, to assist in the extrication of victims. Some work on removing windows, others on the removal of the roof to allow the intervention and protection of the victims of the accident.

Paramedics try to find their way to a delicate approach to minimize injury during the extrication and to take care of those that result in the disaster. Qualified medical rescuers hold oxygen masks, patient triage and without much ado they use initial medical assessment of the patient by qualified medical rescuers.

Numerous victims were trapped inside their cars, others thrown on the pavement. Anand had to be carried out after they extricated the door that was jammed, with the Jaws of life. He looked completely battered and covered with blood.

There were numerous casualties. They remove one victim after the other carefully respecting the head, neck, and back and the axis back assuring the rectitude of the spine when they transfer the victims to the ambulance. The EMS attend to the numerous casualties in this appalling accident

The Paramedics gently move Hailey as she had been flung through the windshield and had lost consciousness. She was surrounded by qualified Medical rescuers.

They put her on a long spine board to immobilize her after they perform the cardiopulmonary resuscitation to try to revive her. They also place an intravenous drip. She has an open penetrating head injury. They press firmly on the wound on the head with gauze to stop the excess bleeding and wrap it with a bandage. They tried asking her questions but there was no answer. She was unconscious, completely covered with cuts and bruises.

In a moment a helicopter lands and she was flown to the nearest hospital.

Other paramedics do the midlevel assessment, stopping the bleeding, putting cervical collars, oxygen and first aid. The EMS perform more detailed medical care. Most of the victims needed an intravenous drip- others cardiopulmonary resuscitation.

Bodies and, body parts, were all scattered among the battered cars. Parts of the cars, and broken glass and all kinds of objects litter the whole area along the highway. The highway was immediately closed.

Most of the drivers were between the ages twenty to thirty. There were numerous deaths but a couple of lucky ones escaped with minor injuries- cuts and bruises all over their body. This was a very sad way to end such a special day.

At the Hospital

The hospital was crowded with devastated, family members. The receptionist was lost to see such an influx of people. The lack of staff, on that special day added to the problem. She tried her best to do what she could, to calm them. But she was in the dark, as it all that happened in the fleeting second on such an auspicious day and she had little or no information whatsoever to communicate with the awaiting, distraught family members.

One of the members from the Spanish Embassy who was sent to meet Hailey after her call, witnessed the scene from afar. They were very fortunate not to have been too close.

They approached the officials and presented their credentials. But they did not mention anything about her call for help, to them. They played diplomacy. They just mentioned that they were expecting one of their citizens arriving in Dubai. This is the call we received. "I am just leaving the airport and will be going directly to the Embassy with no other explanation. Since she did not arrive we came here after we saw the news flash about this deadly accident."

REACTION OF EMBASSY

After they had received her call, they made sure to check on her. They had details of her friends who they contacted immediately. They corroborated with the story. So they realised that Hailey hadn't invented anything.

AZIZ - THE REACTION

*A*ziz hears about the accident and immediately goes to the News Channel. They mentioned that the only female involved in this devastating accident was a young lady who was a foreigner.

He called Sarita and Jumma. They gave him the news that Sarita was missing. He realises that Hailey could have been in the accident, as she could not be seen anywhere. He goes and picks them up and rushes to the hospital.

But nobody was allowed near the patients according to instructions given at the hospital. Hailey was considered a protected citizen of Spain. Only family members were allowed. Since there were none, nobody was allowed. Besides she was in the ICU, fighting between life and death.

The three of them were filled with great sorrow. Tears flow uncontrolled from Jumma and Sarita's faces. They had become very close, they felt as if they were sisters.

AZIZ AT THE HOSPITAL

Alice with her husband stood some distance away. Alice kept sobbing uncontrollably. They were mad the moment they set eyes on Aziz standing there. He tried to approach them but they turned away and made sure to keep a great distance between them. Alice hated him, that's putting it mildly.

Anand's family was also present. The moment he sees them he walked toward them. He deduced that Anand must have involved in the accident as he sees the wife sobbing. Doubtless to say he knew nothing about the connection. Numerous cars had been involved in the collision after they were returning from the Sufi ZICA. Since they were shaken up, all he could do was to give them a hug and move away.

There was pin-drop silence, with the interruption, of now and again a scream or a sob. Most were dumbfounded and still in a shock. An expression of doom covered their faces. They sat patiently waiting to speak to anyone who could give them some information, which wasn't coming due to the heinousness of the situation and the numerous drivers involved. They were all shown to the waiting room. But nobody was allowed to visit any of the patients due to the heinousness of their situation- most of them were in the ICU.

Two hours later one of the doctors approached one of the members, from the Embassy. "It's too, early to give any of you a positive diagnosis. Hailey is fighting between life and death. It is better for you to leave. We will contact you as soon as we feel comfortable that she is well enough to see or communicate with anyone. At the moment she has to be protected, from being contaminated. No visits will be allowed until such time we feel she is safe and above all we have to make sure she wakes up from the coma. The trauma has been very severe. We can't promise you anything but it seems as if she has overcome the first phase. We will do all in our power to help her survive this episode. "

Aziz overhears the conversation between the doctor and the Embassy. He realises he could do nothing there.

NEW ENCOUNTER

Alice turns to see a lady burst into violent sobbing. The doctor was holding her tight.

"We did all we could to save him but the impact was too great. His body was completely trapped by the head –on collision where the front ends of the two cars that came crashing into each other. To make matter worse other cars came crashing from the rear end and side. This created the greatest complication which no driver could survive.

All we can say is he didn't suffer very much as his death was literally instantaneous."

At that time, Alice was unaware of the connection between this lady who was Anand's wife and Hailey. They did not realize that should Hailey come out of all this, it would be thanks to all Anand and his family who had gone out of their way to help free her.

Alice decided to stay at the hospital. She felt she couldn't leave Hailey alone. While waiting she decided to contact Pierre.

"We have found Hailey," she whispered, "I think you should fly out immediately. She is….she is admitted in the hospital aaand is in the… ICU - fighting, between life and death. We have no more information, except that she was involved in multiple car crash."

GHE GURN OF EVENGS

Aziz was completely distraught. Sarita gave him the note Hailey had left back. He was desperate and decided he was going to investigate the matter. He wanted to know who had helped Hailey to leave the hotel.

He began to use his influence firstly by obtaining the capacity to be given all first, hand information about Hailey. But, he wasn't allowed near her, despite his persistence. According to the doctor, no visitors, except family were allowed to see her. But in this situation not even family, could do so as she was in a critical situation. He realises that Hailey was not helped by her friends as he saw them alive and kicking in the hospital. This made him very suspicious.

The Embassy was aware of Aziz and knew that they had to be alert just in case he does make a move to take her out of this hospital to a private one.

They left a security guard behind to make sure that nothing underhand could take place.

But they also realised that it wasn't going to be as easy to protect her from someone who looked as powerful as Aziz. He spread the Aura of power.

His appearance proved that he was suffering a great deal. His hair was all tousled. He kept nervously walking up and down.

He also moved freely amongst the cops, giving them some kind of instructions and giving them the impression that he was the boss. He looked haggard. It was clear that he wanted to do all in his power to help her because he loved her.

ALICE AT THE EMBASSY

*P*ierre arrived the next day. Together Alice accompanied him to the Embassy. He presented his credentials to them. They promised to do all within their power to help.

Once Alice was home, they began with coffee after coffee, discussing ways and means of how they could protect Hailey.

GHE NEW CONNECGION

The next day they receive a note in the mail box. It was a note from Anand's brother.

Amrit wrote: "It is of utmost importance I meet with Hailey's family and friends. I have a secret to reveal. When can we meet? Or could I visit you? Visiting your home may not be the best place."

ԵHE SUSPICION

Aziz calls Sarita and Jumma for a meeting.

"In the note Hailey said her friends had picked her up. But I saw her friends at the hospital and they are perfectly well. How could that be possible when Hailey was in a horrendous accident? Her best friends were at the hospital, in perfect condition. I know her most of them. So who could have picked her up? I do not know she had any connection with the people who have had been involved.

At that moment, he receives a call.

Cops, "All registration plates prove that the owners were mostly young, or people who are citizens of this country. That's the most we can tell you at this moment."

Aziz, "Are you sure there were no foreigners involved in the accident who were drivers?"

Cops, "We are positive about that."

Aziz, "Please let me know who the drivers were and thank you for your kindness to keep me informed."

Later Aziz received a call again.

Cops, "There was a taxi involved in the accident."

Aziz, "So she must have asked the receptionist to call for a cab. So I have to speak to the receptionist." On arriving at the hotel, the first thing he does is to approach the Receptionist.

The receptionist, "As much as I would like to help you, it was too busy a day for me to keep track of all the movement that took place. There were far too many people to attend to, due to the Sufi Zika. Besides just on that day there was an influx of tourists. One of them might have made the call. I was the only one at the desk. I am really very sorry and would have liked to be of help to you sir. But that is impossible. Please forgive me."

Aziz finds himself at a dead end. It seemed impossible to know who had helped her. The cab seemed the only way she could have left. He didn't think any locals had anything to do with her.

Aziz goes to the Police station. He asks for the chief of staff. The moment they saw him they were all reverence. "Good day to you sir, is there anything we could do for you?"

Aziz, "Well I would be pleased if you could give me all the relevant information connected with the deadly accident that took place recently

— Who was who
— In which car each of the casualties, had been travelling with.
— Very specially I would like detailed information about Hailey who is in the ICU, at this moment."

"Sir, as much as we would like to give you that information, at this moment, it is nearly impossible for us to know anything. The impact was so great that bodies were strewn all over the place and most of the cars have been completely destroyed and their plates have been dispersed. Until such time as family members come for information we have nothing to show you, nor help you, in any way, as much as we would like to do so. The moment we know something we will let you know immediately.

Another Official, "You must be aware that this was more than multiple car crash with numerous casualties. No more than three survived, if we can count on Hailey. And they are all in the ICU."

Aziz, "Have you any idea with who Hailey had been driving. That is of vital importance to me. Whoever he or she is, they are responsible for her present situation.

A couple of hours later, Aziz joined the numerous families who were patiently sitting in the waiting room. Most of them looked shattered. All of them, requesting details of their families.

The officials were at a loss for words. "Rest assured, the moment we know anything, we will publish it in the papers and also notify each of you who come here. Remember to leave your contact details with the receptionist.

THE REVELATION

Alice thought the best place to meet would have to be at the Embassy. She was sure that Aziz would keep a watch over her house.

Amrit, Anand's brother meets them at the Embassy.

After the introductions were made, Amrit showed them the note that Hailey had given his brother.

"My brother was responsible for rescuing Hailey from Aziz, at her request. But I assure you he wasn't responsible for her accident, as you must have read about this disaster where I lost my brother. He was a very big-hearted person always ready to help anyone in need." He turns away as a sob escaped him.

I don't know if you were aware that she was held captive under false pretences to begin with.

Needless to say that Aziz was madly in love with her and gave her, the very best. She was part of his Harem but he treated her in a special way. After her arrival he only had time for her, we were told.

But she wasn't happy, she just wanted to go home. She was really very brave to take the step to ask my brother for help. She was fortunate to have gone to the right person. In these circumstances nobody would have taken the risk to do so. It was nearly impossible to escape from where she was living. They were always under vigilance.

I have lost a great brother. He is the husband of the lady you saw sobbing in the hospital. But it would have been disastrous for the whole family had he been alive and discovered to have been the one who helped Hailey out. Aziz is a very powerful man.

Above all I am here to warn you. You can count on us, should you need any help. Nobody should be aware of what exactly happened at the accident. Most of the crucial players are dead. You should make sure that you are going to be the first persons to talk to her when she gets out of her coma. Alice sobs. Don't worry she will come out of this. I am sure!

My brother had a flourishing business at the Souk where Hailey and her friends, used to shop. When she realised she could trust him, she requested him to help her out of the prison, where she felt trapped with no way out. He agreed to do so and actually, bought her ticket to Spain. You must have received her bags that were checked directly to Spain.

He had dropped her off at the airport, but had to pick her up again when her flight was cancelled due to severe weather conditions.

He stammers, then stops as tears flow from his eyes.....and now we have lost him through no fault of his.

Alice hugs him. She realises that Hailey could not have escaped on her own. His wife asked if she could meet you. She also played a very important part.

STRANGE EPISODE

The security guard was just dozing off when he thought he heard some movement. He turned to see someone who looked like a nurse but his strange behaviour drew his attention– as he kept turning around all the time, looking left, right and centre before he approached Hailey's room.

The guard was a trained nurse, too. He follows the nurse inside, "Oh! I am sorry am I in the right room? I am supposed to give Hailey an injection. Maybe either of us could have made a mistake. I am new here."

Yes I am sure you did. Let me check. He pretends to check and pretends to accidently crash into him dropping all the contents of the tray. But out comes the needle he had in his hand, the security guard catches him off guard and sticks the needle into his thigh. He falls flat on the floor. He presses a button on his telephone. And moves swiftly to unplug all the tubes connected with Hailey. There was a secret connecting with the room, so she was wheeled to the next room. They locked the room so nobody could enter without a key.

They waited for a few moments and soon heard a phone ring which belonged to the intruder. It was followed by footsteps rushing into the room. They left the intruder on the floor and rushed towards the lifts. There were two of them. One ran towards the stairs. expecting that somebody would follow up

Milton Keynes UK
Ingram Content Group UK Ltd.
UKHW031900260924
448786UK00001B/121

9 781964 744575